Sleepy Hollow

Original Tales of Terror from America's Spookiest Village

Edited by David Neilsen

NEILSEN BOOKS

ISBN:1514838966
ISBN-13:978-1514838969

To the people of Sleepy Hollow.

God help you.

THE LEGENDS

A Most Appropriate Forward--Washington Irving   4

The White Lady of Raven Rock--Jonathan Kruk   7

By This Candle's Light--Christine Morgan   13

The Devil's Spindle--Scott J Laurange   30

Passing Through--James C. Simpson   48

Mayflies--Ezra Heilman   61

A Local Superstition--B. B. Stucco   74

Dead Men Rise--Andrew M. Seddon   80

The Secret of Pendlewood Court--Michael Nayak   102

Hell to Pay--Amy Bruan   125

The Dying Dream of Major Andre--Robert Stava   145

Within Reach--David Neilsen   163

Those Responsible   173

A Most Appropriate Forward

By Washington Irving

Well it is that I should be asked to render my thoughts upon the volume you hold in your clammy hands. There be not a shred of doubt this untoward compilation owes its very existence to mine most acknowledged and agreeable work, that being the trials and tribulations of a certain vainglorious-if-overly-peckish schoolmaster. Point of fact, the very title of this lexicon apes that storied tale, and one would not be reticent to look toward legal recompense over the sullied matter if one thought it worth either time or material investment.

That the publishers have attempted to mollify the indignity with an invitation to comment on the fruit of their labors is, I will admit, a shrewd gesture. It was with a wary eye, therefore, that I did dive into the questionable literature herein.

God help me, but my purview of the pages beneath your undoubtedly sweaty fingers did bring a smile to my face and a twinkle to mine eye. The tranquil settings of Sleepy Hollow and its environs have long cast a spell o'er me. Well aware am I that the legacy of ghosts and ghouls which doth persist in this mesmerizing region yet lends itself to myriad tales, of which mine is but a single example--albeit by far the most engrossing and professionally recorded. Glad I was to lose myself once again within this deceptively lazy setting whilst phantoms not of my own making traipsed across the page. Truly, it is an enchanted land which is nestled on the eastern bank of the mighty Hudson in the crook of the Tappan Zee. A land filled with wonder, mystery, and a perilous connection to that other world existing in the corner of one's mind's eye, just out of range of vision.

While none of the selections contained within can hold a candle to my own master work of similar title, they are not without their individual charms. They range in topic from that woeful creature of Raven Rock to the secrets of the grave to the perils of gluttony, yet one element

4

intertwines itself throughout each episode: the ever-present, ever-ominous power of Sleepy Hollow, itself.

That my name shall forever be associated with this blessed-yet-damned locale I acknowledge and, indeed, relish. Having had the forethought to copyright any and all literary mention of said village, I have carefully vetted each and every iteration which has followed mine own superior encapsulation. Thus have I been able to maintain the atmosphere of dread and shudder which is invoked by mere utterance of the storied village's name.

Though I take no responsibility for the Tim Burton film. Honestly, Ichabod, an investigator? The man hadn't the grey matter to investigate his shoes, much less a supernatural conspiracy consisting of demon trees, ancient curses, and Christopher Walken.

But I digress.

The legends of Sleepy Hollow are many. Those recounted on the following pages but scratch the surface of the dooms and glooms which have visited this region since time immemorial. Spirits dance in the streets. Goblins hide in the trees. Monsters lurk in the shadows. And reigning over them all, The Horseman waits with his loathsome blade, itching to sever another grimacing trophy from atop an unlucky passersby's shoulders and add it to his gruesome collection.

That's just how they roll in Sleepy Hollow.

Author Washington Irving enjoys a fresh margarita on the shores of the mighty Hudson whilst contemplating life's cruel ironies.

The White Lady
of Raven Rock

Adapted by Jonathan Kruk

There moans a chilling voice at times over the Hudson River's Tappan Zee. It portends of a coming storm, and tells of a forlorn spirit. Gather you near now, and listen to the legend of The White Lady of Raven Rock.

British troopers after the battle of White Plains, sought out houses along the shores of the Hudson to await their orders. Two Redcoated officers appeared on the stoop of a rough hewn home here in Sleepy Hollow. The younger, a handsome lieutenant, went to knock, but his superior, a gruff Major stopped him.

"Leftenant, just open the door and enter this colonial cottage - no need to give a knock. Watch me!" The Major lifted the latch. The pair tromped in, mud and manure falling from their boots.

"By the power granted to us soldiers of his majesty George the Third, we, your protectors from Washington and his rebel mob, will be quartered in this house." The major announced. "Come forward and be of service to your King!"

No one appeared.

"Major, some one is about, see the fireplace is ablaze."

"COME FORWARD AND SERVE YOUR PROTECTORS!"

Now, behind a flour barrel trembled a young woman, her name may have been Priscilla. She hoped the officers upon seeing her humble home would leave. Recalling how other Westchester homes had been burned by the British army, she wisely came out from her hiding.

"Forgive me sir, I am much afeared!"

"Nothing to fear save those rebels!" exclaimed the Major. "Now, be of some service. Remove our boots, then prepare us a meal."

Priscilla gripped the major's filthy boots, and pulled them off. The Leftenant, noticed her delicate hands, beautiful, even covered in mud. "I shall remove my own boots outside. No sense in dirtying your home all the more."

Priscilla smiled at the Leftenant. "I've only hasty pudding and bread to offer."

"Well, fetch us some, my lass! The major ordered. "At least 'tis better than Saint Anthony's meal!"

"Are you here alone?" the Leftenant asked.

"Yeah, Sir, my brothers both fight in this war, though one fights the for King."

The Leftenant smiled back at Priscilla. And thus began their love.

Now, the commander of these two Redcoat officers was a General named Howe. How he fought was like a slow game of chess. Once Washington moved his army, Howe would sit and think, then cautiously move his army. This made for long waits, which gave the Leftenant time with his Sleepy Hollow lady.

The two spent hours strolling along the shores of the Tappan Zee, talking of times of peace. The Leftenant explained 'My family owns a sugar plantation on the warm island of Jamaica. Only sweet sun shines there, never a war!"

"Perhaps, you shall bring me there to see it! I am weary of the war and Westchester."

"Perhaps!" the Leftenant smiled.

The Major just laughed at the younger officer and told him "enjoy your colonial wench, for soon we all will march and, perhaps, die!"

Priscilla's neighbors, did not see any joy in her falling for a British officer.

The blacksmith told alewife in the Tarrytown tavern one afternoon "I found the two of them behind me shop, holding hands!"

"That's a trifle!" the alewife replied. "I found the two of them a-kissing!"

Both agreed no good will come from this love!

One day, there came to the door of Priscilla's cottage, a messenger from General Howe.

"Sirs, you are hereby ordered to report to Dobbs Ferry to pursue Washington and his rebels in New Jersey."

"Well, there we have it, Leftenant: the war beckons!" the Major cried.

"You'd best kiss your wench farewell! And kiss her once for me!"

The Leftenant dashed off to find his love. "Please, Priscilla, leave your chores and come with me!"

"Why, pray tell?"

"You shall see!"

The Leftenant led Priscilla from the gloom of Sleepy Hollow, above the Pocantico Hills, to a craggy bluff known as Raven Rock. "Look, my Priscilla, see the wide waters of the Tappan Zee!"

"Yeah, my beloved, I see the to the Cliffs of the Palisades. But why are we here?"

The Leftenant answered by getting on bended knee, taking Priscilla's hand, and begging "wilt thou marry me? And know this: I shall leave the service of the King to sail here to take thee away to Jamaica where we shall enjoy only peace."

Priscilla kissed both of her love's cheeks and answered. "Yes! I shall marry thee. I will make a gown of white and await you here!"

"Splendid," cried the Leftenant. "Come in two months time when my service is done. I shall sail through the Tappan Zee to Tarrytown. Look for my white topsail!"

The couple departed, with a last kiss, believing themselves safe by love.

The Leftenant joined General Howe, and how they fought against George Washington and his Blue Coats!

The young woman gathered scraps of white, wool, linen and linsey-woolsey. She pieced and sewed her wedding gown.

The Blacksmith warned. "Lass, your brothers, neither the redcoat nor bluecoat, will approve of your loving a British officer! He will just steal your kisses!

The alewife scolded "If that Leftenant comes, it will only be to break your heart. He'll leave you crying!"

Priscilla answered fiercely. "Nay, my love is true. It will endure!"

When two months passed, Priscilla, appeared in a patchwork gown of white on Raven Rocks, peering out over the Tappan Zee. She spied not her beloved's white sail, but the first storm of winter. Steely clouds amassed over the Palisades, white caps raged on the Hudson River, winds pushed bitter winds and icy snow toward Raven Rock.

Priscilla, hoping for her love, saw the foamy waves as waving white sail. She called "My beloved! Is that you? Have you come for me?"

Only the stinging snows and biting winds answered.

Priscilla, looked out again. More white caps appeared. Could that be a sloop sail? Again the lass, though freezing, called "My beloved! Is that you? Have you come for me?"

Only the stinging snows and biting winds answered.

Still, Priscilla stayed on Raven Rocks. The winds pushed through her gown. The snows stung her cheeks, blistered bloody her lips, and bit her delicate beautiful hands raw with frost. Searching for her love, crying till her voice was hoarse. "My beloved! Is that you? Have you come for me?"

Only the stinging snows and biting winds answered.

The course of true love, a wise Bard wrote, never did run smooth! Where was the leftenant? Dead on a New Jersey battle field? Some claimed the Major locked him up rather than "let one of my officers run off with a rebellious Yankee Doodle Wench!"

When morning came, the White Lady was gone. Had her beloved come? Or had the snow and war swept her away? When her brothers returned to Sleepy Hollow, the alewife explained. "Your sister's gone! Perhaps the Leftenant took her to New York."

But the Blacksmith added. "If he did, he stole her kisses and broke her heart!" Alas, where was this white lady of Sleepy Hollow?

Spring gave the answer. Two huntsmen hoping to find rabbit found instead a strange misshaped site. "Looky thar! Wha' tis it me friend? I dunno, but we'd best fetch the dominie. Dashing down from Raven Rock, they burst into the old Dutch Church, the very same from whence the Headless Horseman now rides. "Dominie, Dominie, come quick to Raven Rock. We found someone! Bring your Good Book. The good man grabbed his bible and followed the hunters.

There amidst the melting snows, the Dominie clapped eyes upon a wretched sight.

"Who is this? Do I know? Are those not the hands that once removed a British trooper's filthy boots? Now the knuckles stick through the skin. Those cheeks once looked like peaches, flush with love. Now they hang frozen and torn. Those lips, purple and blistered, once spoke only of love!" Alas, this once was the dear woman who loved a British officer. She must have awaited him here through the blizzard. Only death came for her at Raven Rock. Come men, help me bury her by the old stone church."

They laid the Lady in White's body to rest. But her forlorn spirit remains restless. Rising just before storms, the White Lady returns to haunt Raven Rock. Why? The answer is found in the Dominie's Good Book. There is says "Love is as strong as death!"

You shall see how strong. Look here and listen. Through the mists and gloom of Sleepy Hollow, the White Lady still moans, her voice caught in the wind, her spirit still calling....

"My beloved, is that you? Have you come for me? My Beloved, is that you?"

BY THIS CANDLE'S LIGHT

By Christine Morgan

By this light, this candle's light
Now show me fair and true
What waits?
What fates?
What secrets hide?
What do I wish I knew?

In hooded cloaks, with whispered giggles, the three girls hastened down the lane.

An autumn dusk had fallen. Woodsmoke filled the air, and the scent of apples crisp and ripe. Dry leaves rustled on their boughs or rested deep in drifts beneath the trees. Down along the river, the night-fog might be rising, but the skies above were clear.

Pretty Betje Van Klaas led the way, her eyes – blue as the twilight – bright with excitement, her steps quick and eager. At seventeen, she was the eldest. Like her sister and cousin, she had hair of butter-blonde, though her cheeks were rosier, her face and figure more becoming.

"-- which one," she said. "Ernst and Jakob are each so handsome, but there's much to be said for Otto as well --"

"In other words, he's rich," Tess whispered to Annika, and giggled again. "Almost as rich as Father."

"What's important," Betje went on, as if she hadn't heard, "is that they all want to marry me, and I don't know how to choose."

When Pietr Van Klaas had announced his intention to stay a week or more in Tarry Town for his business dealings, the girls had beseeched him to bring them along. And he, thinking they had eyes for new frocks or bonnets, indulgently agreed.

He of course had no idea they'd slip from the inn on a more daring and mysterious adventure.

Whither to, whither to, candle-bird

Smoke-grey, blue, and black
White as wick new-twisted
Quick the yellow fire-bright
Whither to, I follow where
Whither to, I gather there
Boil, berry, boil, fifteen into one
Skim the sweet wax-myrtle
Now the spell is done

They say John Wickburn brought her home with him from somewhere away. Somewhere north along the rocky coasts, where waves crash and foam leaps high, where more men are lost each year to the cold sea than to the dark woods. Farport, it was, or Ipswich, or Devil's Cove; no one seems to know.

If his family might have opposed the match, well, they were 'most gone by then. And he, himself, always was an odd one. Nose forever in his books. Scholarly, you see, learned, but not the sort to become clerk or clergyman, or pursue medicine or law. No great wonder he should seek a wife far from the valley.

And they say she was good for him. That they were well-suited.

A shame it was, then, such a shame, how terribly he died.

"Won't Uncle Pietr be cross with us?" asked Annika.

They'd left behind the shops and houses of the village square, the lane passing now through farmers' fields where cornstalks shifted and pumpkins grew fat and round. Ahead, it wended on toward a dale of whispering woods, known to some as Sleepy Hollow.

"Oh, he needn't know. He'll be at the tavern late." Betje spoke with the carefree confidence of a favored child; one who knew full well that, no matter her transgressions, forgiveness would dotingly be granted.

Annika, whose own parents were long in the grave and whose brother had foisted her off on their more prosperous relations, envied that confidence greatly. Even more, perhaps, than she envied Betje's beauty, fine dresses, and vying suitors.

Her own prospects in that regard were rather scarce. But perhaps, and who knew, this scheme of her cousin's might also bring her some hope, insight, and guidance.

Or perhaps not. Perhaps it was nothing more than silliness and superstition, a way to trick the gullible out of a bit of money.

Well, if so, so be it. Betje had money and to spare. If she chose to fritter it on purported magic charms, then let her. Was it any less frivolous than buying sweetmeats and silken ribbons?

"Besides," added Betje with a toss of her head, dislodging her hood to fall back on her shoulders, "Old Mag will keep our secret."

It had been Old Mag to tell the girls of the candle-maker's widow, just as it had been Old Mag to tell them of the little hill-men playing ninepins, haunted mills and standing stones, the Yellow Man of the Woods, and countless other tales.

Stories upon stories, and lore upon lore. The meanings of dreams, what brought good luck or bad, how to banish freckles with lemon-water and cure headaches with a silver spoon … there was no end to Old Mag's wisdom.

Yet here, now, in the gloaming, Annika wondered if wisdom it truly was.

Behold the holy Lamb of God,
The Calf, the Cow, the Sheep
Behold the butcher's bounty
Meat and mutton, milk to keep
Behold the hide, the hoof, the horn
The rendered kitchen's trim
Into light, deliver us from darkness
Into grace, deliver us from sin

Her name, if ever I heard, I can't remember. The chandleress, folk called her, or just John Wickburn's wife. It wasn't that she was disliked; it wasn't that she was feared. She kept to herself, was all. They both did. Kept to themselves and to each other.

Oh, they'd go to market, and to church a'Sundays, and when there came a wedding or a funeral, a christening or a fair, they'd turn up like as not. But they weren't ones to take tea or supper with the neighbors. She wasn't one to gossip in the square, and he, he wasn't one to tarry at the tavern.

And of course they made and sold their candles.
Candles of all kinds.

Shadows hung around them like soft drapes. Ground-mist crept in the low hollows. The nearest farmhouse stood a quarter-mile away. Even to girls accustomed to country-quiet as they were, the evening held a strange and somnolent hush.

"Are there Indians?" Tess peered around, not afraid, but curious.

Her sister scoffed. "Indians? Why not bears?"

"*Are* there bears?" Annika hugged herself.

"Don't be a ninny-goose. We're perfectly safe. Come along. Old Mag said the path turns off just past the bridge."

Sure enough, they soon came to a wooden bridge. The rocky stream it spanned flowed, chuckling, toward the river. There, they paused, giggles and whispers ceasing. Even Betje seemed, for a moment, unsure.

"I see something on the other side," said Tess. "A light … there, do you see it?"

"I do," Annika said. "I think it's a candle."

"Well, then!" Betje's uncertainty melted like frost against a warm windowpane. Reaching out, laughing merrily, she clasped one of their hands in each of hers and drew them forward.

Their footfalls sounded too loud upon the weathered planks as they crossed, making them glance over their shoulders as if the echoing noise might have upset some fellow travelers. There were, of course, no others out and about. Cool wisps of vapor wafted upward from the burbling water.

The flicker of light they'd glimpsed grew stronger. The candle – for, indeed, candle it was; squat and thick, of yellow tallow giving off its oily, fatty smell – had been set into the sunken top of an old and rotted stump.

"This must be the way," said Betje, nodding at a narrow path leading past the stump. It looked to follow twist for turn the course upstream. Along it, at uneven intervals, other small lights winked and glimmered, a line of tiny beacons wending deeper into denser groves.

The second candle, some dozen paces further on, sat atop a rounded stone. The third sprouted as if like a waxy mushroom from the bole of a fallen log.

In underbrush and shadows, night-creatures rustled. The vast wide eyes of a moon-owl glinted from the high fork of a tree. Moths flitted and whirled.

Their steps, ordinary on the road and loud upon the bridge, were all but silent on the loamy earth. A renewed anticipation thrilled in each girl's heart. These candles, this trail of flickering flames, proved the first part of Old Mag's story. There *was* a path, going somewhere, and a path not left untended. Surely something must be at the end of it.

> *Sun and soil, wind and rain*
> *Let the springtime come again*
> *Field and flower, marsh and fen*
> *Wild meadow, tamed garden*
> *Clover waving in green seas*
> *Apple blossoms in the trees*
> *Aster, bluebells, white poppies*
> *To them all, come flock the bees*
> *Gather, gather, nectar sweet*
> *Buzz and bumble as we meet*
> *Fill the hives a golden treat*
> *Sumptuous for a queen to eat*
> *Drain'ed out the honeycomb*
> *Strain'ed off the slumgum foam*
> *Candles make to light the home*
> *And in shadows no more roam*

Of all kinds ... she'd go often into the woods with a basket on her arm to pick bayberries, bayberries to boil for their myrtle-wax ... odd of nature though he might be, John Wickburn was on good terms with the butchers, who saved aside for him at a fair price the kidney-suet for rendering into tallow; the poorest families could afford no better ... and beeswax, of course.

Some they poured and some they dipped. Some they carved or moulded. For the churches, magistrates and schoolmasters, some were made with hour-markings to track the time.

And then there were the other candles.

Those most particular, and special.

It felt they had been hours on the path, although Annika knew it could not be so long. What showed of the sky beyond the branch-crossed canopies was a rich violet-blue, with only the first bright star-points shining in it like jewels against a gown.

With the way so narrow, they'd unclasped hands and gone on single-file, Betje in the lead with Tess at her heels, and Annika herself bringing up the rear. Now she paused and looked back, trying to guess how far they'd come.

Her breath caught in her throat. At her gasp, the others turned.

"What is it?" Tess asked. "What's the matter?"

"The candles," Annika said. "The lights behind us, they're gone."

"We just can't see them through the trees," said Betje.

"No; they've disappeared! They've gone out!"

"The wind, then."

"There's hardly wind to speak of!"

"The ones ahead of us still burn," Tess said.

Betje shrugged. "Well, then, we go on."

"Go on? Are you certain?" asked Annika.

"We can't very well go back."

"We could follow along the stream --"

"I don't hear the stream," said Tess. "Do you?"

They listened, but the rushing chuckle of the water was nowhere to be heard. The path had veered from it, and the direction in which Annika thought it must lay was a thick tangle of brush and brambles.

It seemed Betje was right and they had no choice but to press on. Others of Old Mag's tales – will'o'wisps, spirit lanterns, fairy-fires dancing with glowflies – filled Annika's mind. But these? Each candle as they came to it proved normal enough. If each one somehow vanished once they'd gone by ...

"Look," Tess said. "Look there, a clearing, and a cottage."

So there was, a cottage in a clearing, a neat cottage with a stick-fenced garden and a shallow stone-ringed well out front. Threads of smoke curled from the chimney. Beside it were some smaller outbuildings – a cow-shed, a chicken coop.

Upon the cottage stoop clustered several lit candles of every shape and size and color. Melted wax from them ran together as it puddled and congealed.

More candle-light from within showed through an open shutter. A large grey cat sat on the sill, washing its face. It stopped with one paw held up as the girls entered the yard. An ear flicked as if to dislodge a fly. The tip of its tail twitched. It watched them with eyes more lambent than those of the moon-owl, then sprang down inside the cottage.

Betje urged the others with a look and a motion of her head, and approached. Annika and Tess clasped hands again, and followed.

At the door, Betje knocked.

A moment later, it opened.

Keep this house in happiness, bar trouble from the door
Keep love and laughter in your light, for now, forevermore
Let no misfortune come here, no sickness, pain, or grief
Let times of trial pass us by, and our discomforts be brief
May all who dwell beneath this roof live long in good health
May we share the happiness of friendship's richest wealth

Such rare, strange, wonderful candles! Crafted with seeds and dyes, and scented oils ... they might have coins embedded in them, bits of metal, tacks, or silver pins, or nails. Crushed herbs and petals from dried flowers. Any of a thousand things, for a thousand purposes.

The wicks were twisted not only from rush-reeds or cotton, but from threads of cloth – a bridal veil, a winding shroud, the sheets of a nuptial bed, a child's christening gown. Or from horsetails, feather-down, even strands of hair.

Candles red as heart's blood, green as new leaves, black as night.

And as dear as the cost might be, folk would pay, and gladly.

There stood at the threshold a pale and slender woman-wraith.

Her flesh seemed carved from polished ivory, her features as smooth and serene as a cameo on a brooch. Her brow was high, her nose narrow, her chin pointed. Her eyes were slightly uptilted, very large, and very dark.

She wore her hair unbound, uncovered by any kerchief. It fell straight and smooth and fine as silk to her slim shoulders. Its color was – most of all in a county well-known for blondes buttery or flaxen, for towheads and redheads, and for locks of amber wheat and nutty brown – remarkable in its blackness.

And more remarkable yet in its streaks of soot-grey and ashy-white, for the woman standing before them did otherwise not look much older than did Betje, herself.

No surprise or curiosity showed in her visage as she looked upon the three girls on her stoop, only that calm serenity. Her dress and apron were simple, the latter spotted here and there with dried drips of wax.

For a moment, none of them spoke. Then Betje asked, "Are you the Widow Wickburn?"

"I am she," said the pale woman. Her voice was cool and low.

"We have heard," said Betje, "that you make candles."

"Yes, that I do."

"Candles of … rare kinds."

The widow smiled. "I make candles of many kinds."

"But some," Betje persisted, "we're told some are special."

"They all are special." The faint, small smile still played about her lips.

Betje's own lips pressed together. Her cheeks pinked, but her gaze never wavered. Finally, her throat moved as she swallowed. She lifted her chin in daring.

"*Magic* candles," she said at last.

"Ah. And who told you such things?"

"Old Mag, a servant in the household of my father, Pietr Van Klaas."

"Old Mag." She seemed to turn the name over in her mind. "Who are these young ladies with you?"

"My sister and our cousin."

"Well. Perhaps you should come in."

Safe travels upon road or sea
Wherever you may roam
Burning will this candle be
Until you've safe come home
And if death should take you first
May its light snuff out
So that I will know the worst
And linger not in doubt

*No one much talks of it openly, of course. Word passes in rumor, or in secret trust, mouth-to-ear. More among women than the menfolk of the valley – not for reasons of hen's gossip but because these are for the most part **our** concerns. Home and hearth, heart and health, you see.*

Which is not to say no men knew, or know. Or bother with such things. Some do. And why not? Many of their wishes and desires are not so different. Luck and love, profit and prosperity.

And business, mostly business. Man's business, they'd call it.

While ours remained women's work.

Inside, the cottage proved to be warm and cozy. Its main room glowed in the light of many candles as well as that of a fireplace. Suspended over the coals on an iron arm, a boiling pot issued thin whistles of bayberry-smelling steam from under its lid. Shelves above and beside the fireplace served as both pantry and sideboard.

The cat, which they'd seen in the window, regarded them from the lid of a chest at the foot of a quilt-covered bed. Its eyes, no longer eerily lambent, were bright copper coins. Half its face was scarred, drawn up in what looked like a sneer.

"There are coat-pegs on the walls, and stools under the table," said Widow Wickburn, "if you care to make yourselves comfortable. Might I offer you some tea?"

"Thank you, that would be very kind." Betje slipped off her cloak and hung it on a peg; the others followed her example.

Annika gazed at their surroundings. Two doorways, partly blocked by hanging blankets, led off into other, smaller rooms. Through one, she saw what she surmised was a chandler's work-table; the floorboards beneath it were strewn with snips of wicking and blobs of wax. Through the other, she could see nothing but part of a painted canvas floorcloth done in an unusual pattern.

Soon, they were sipping cups of strongly-flavored tea. Tess and Annika nibbled at hard, round honey-cookies, while the chandleress moved her boiled bayberries from the heat and set the pot aside to cool.

"Has your cat a name?" Tess asked.

"Singe-Whisker." She laughed gently as she sat on the edge of the bed. "He was, as a kitten, too inquisitive for his own good."

"Oh, the poor dear creature!"

"It did teach him his lesson." Her pale hand, with its exceptionally long and graceful fingers, stroked along the cat's spine. He arched and stretched the way cats did, rumbling a purr. "And he's quite good company otherwise, when not getting into mischief. He sees spirits, you know."

"Spirits?" The three girls gasped as one.

"Ghosts and magic and much else invisible to us." She scratched Singe-Whisker behind the ears. "Most cats do."

Annika didn't want to ask, but heard herself ask it just the same. "Are you … a witch, then?"

The chandleress smiled. "Isn't that why you came to me?"

In a dish of hammered metal place one tall of yellow wax
Studded all throughout its length with pins and new brass tacks
Light the wick and let it burn
As it melts they fall and fall, a clinking tinkling din
Away from it will evil turn
And if done to me a'purpose by some spell or curse or hex
Revert upon the caster, my enemies to plague and vex

Not so unlike our own old ways, is it, after all? Who does not know to toss a pinch of salt, or to never leave a hat upon the bed? Who does not know that to kill a spider will bring rain? We flip coins and pitch pebbles, we read omens in the tea-dregs; why not drip hot wax into cold water, as children pour sweet-sap or molasses into snow, to see what shapes it takes?

Is it so strange, then, to find wisdom in wax and wick, in flame and smoke? When we nail horseshoes above our doors, why not a candle to ward off the spirits of the dead? Or spit forth sparks whene'er someone lies within their presence?

But the churchmen, and the doctors ... learned men of sciences and faith ...

At best, they called it foolishness and superstition. At best.

Betje put down her cup. "So, it *is* true, then, what Old Mag told us?"

"Perhaps. What did she say?"

"Well ..." She blushed her prettiest, a blush capable of making grown men stammer like schoolboys. "I want to know whom I should wed."

"Of course. Always an important, and difficult, decision."

"I've tried with apples," Betje went on, "reciting the alphabet as I twist the stem, but it breaks off at a different letter every time. And when I pare the peel in a single long piece, to toss behind me, when I turn to look, it never seems to form the same letter twice either. I've also swung a ring on a string around a glass of water, slept with pieces of bride's cake under my pillow, plucked daisy-petals ..."

Widow Wickburn nodded, her expression solemn with understanding.

"Which is why Old Mag said I should ask you," continued Betje. "She said nearly all the women in the valley have come to you for advice one time or another, on everything from sweethearts and husbands to having babies --"

"Yes!" Tess cut in, excited. "She told us that before I was born, the midwife passed one of your candles over Mother's belly and knew I'd be a girl, just from the way the smoke rose!"

"I do much business with midwives, yes. Midwives, young wives, old wives, mothers, grandmothers, brides-to-be ..."

"Well, I *want* to be a bride-to-be! But it must be the right decision. I need to know which one to choose."

"How many suitors do you have?"

Again, Betje blushed most prettily. "Three. Ern--"

"No, do not speak their names. Tell me nothing more of them just now."

"So, you *can* help?"

"If you wish to pursue this, yes, I do believe you'll find some answers. Whether you'll find them to your liking or not, well, that remains yet to be seen."

"I don't care," said Betje, again lifting her chin. "I want to know."

"For a price," Tess prompted in a murmur. "Best ask that as well, 'fore you agree to too much, sister-mine."

"Pff." Betje flapped a hand as if to shoo away an irksome fly. She tossed a little cloth purse onto the table, where it clinked coin-music. "Will this suffice?"

By this light, this candle's light
Now show me fair and true
What waits?
What fates?
What secrets hide?
What do I wish I knew?

There never was any great outcry or accusations ag'inst them; on that count let be clear. Hardly like what went on in Massachusetts some sixty-sevn'ty years ago, with the gallows and the hangings, young girls having fits and so on ... no, none of that.

And folk here, folk from the valley, church and villager alike, had n'owt to do with John Wickburn dying as he did. Well, not as such ... not directly ... not the living ... and no known earthly soul wished him harm.

*He died **saving** those boys at the graveyard, who'd gone there a'midnight on a dare – what, haven't I told you that story?*

Ah, then, another time.

The chandleress had brought out three wax tapers, as pale and slender as her own fingers. Around each, she'd wrapped a strand of Betje's butter-blonde hair sunwise, then a thread from the sleeve of Betje's dress widdershins. She laid flat the mirror'd glass like a tray upon a table. Its surface was unblemished but for the three moist kiss-marks Betje had pressed to it; on each of these, she placed one of the candles.

Annika and Tess exchanged an apprehensive glance from an out-of-the-way corner, where the cat Singe-Whisker curled purring around their ankles. The other flames all had been extinguished, and a standing iron guard unfolded in front of the hearth to block the coals' red glow.

"Here, the first," said the chandleress. "Watch, now. Watch and see."

They'd half-expected to witness the wick spark and kindle at a mere wave of the woman's hand, but she used instead a smolder. The first of the three candles blazed like a small, fierce sun.

"Watch and see," she repeated. Her low, cool voice took on a soothing, almost singing tone. "*The priest, the feast, the nuptial day, the newly-wedded man and wife. To their house they go together to begin their married life.* Do you see?"

Tess raised inquiring eyebrows at Annika, who shrugged and shook her head. She saw only the amorphous play of light and shadow, flickering, dancing on the wall.

"Yes, I see, I do see," Betje said, speaking as one half-roused from a deep sleep. Her gaze was both dreamlike and unwavering, staring as if at some clever pantomime. "The house ... it is a fine house ... yet so quiet, so empty ... where are the children? Are there to be no children? Oh, oh no, it cannot be. We are well-to-do, we are respected ... as we grow old alone us two ... no children for us to raise, no grandchildren to look forward to ..." Her breath hitched.

Over the lit candle, high enough to catch the smoke but not be charred, the chandleress thrice slowly passed a scrap of paper. She then set it aside, blew out the flame, and repeated the ritual with another candle.

"And here, the second. What, now, do you see?"

"A smaller house … less fine, but full … filled with children … my sweet babies … but why are there … horses? cannons? armies and guns? … warships on the river … militia in the woods … no! oh, no! … he's shot! he falls! he dies! … what am I to do? on my own with so many children!" Stricken tears spilled down her cheeks.

Again, the chandleress passed a scrap of paper over the candle, and blew it out. "Here, the third," she said. "By its light, what do you see?"

For a long while, Betje was silent.

Then, she shrieked.

In my hand is held the candle
From the wick issues the flame
Above the flame, the paper
The smoke to write the name

We did often wonder, though, why she stayed after he died. Some as thought sure she'd go back to her own people, from wherever she'd come. True, she had her chandling, and did not lack for business, but the world can be unkind to a widow on her own, without close friends or kin.

All she'd say when asked was that her work here was far from done … that there were evils in Sleepy Hollow as yet unrevealed.

At the shriek, Annika and Tess jumped, clinging to one another and stifling their own cries. Singe-Whisker, his tail puffed, dashed under the bed.

Betje leaped up, whirling, lashing out all about herself with wild arms. She pulled at her hair, tore at her clothes. In her panic, the stool crashed over. So too did the table, sending the mirror'd glass to shatter on the floor and candles rolling askew in all directions. The lit one whiffed out in a splatter of melted wax. Its smoke spun upward in thin, dissipating tendrils.

The chandleress stooped for it with another scrap of paper in her hand, but must not have been quick enough for whatever she intended. Her serene expression briefly became a scowl and she hissed the way even the cat had not.

"Whores and harlots!" Betje wailed. "He has whores and harlots in the city, women, other women! And when he … when he … finishes with them … he … no one knows … no one guesses or suspects … until … until *I* do, and ..."

Her eyelids fluttered. She coughed and gasped and clawed at her own throat before collapsing in a swoon.

"Betje!" Tess ran to her, patting at her cheeks. "She's fainted dead away!"

Annika looked at the chandleress. If she'd had any notions herself of trying these divinations – not that she could afford even a single such candle, she was sure – they had by now been quite scuttled.

What hope was there for the likes of *her*, when rich and pretty *Betje's* fortunes ended in despair? When the best choices Betje had were between lifelong empty childlessness and early widowed motherhood? Not to mention the third choice, which was no choice at all!

It was better *not* to know!

Or … was it?

Couldn't Betje now, forewarned and forearmed, marry *none* of them? Marry someone else, instead?

The chandleress, meanwhile, held the two remaining smoke-marked paper scraps. She studied them, mouth set, face pensive. She glanced at Annika with eyes deep and darkly thoughtful.

"Do you know the names of your cousin's suitors?" she asked.

"Will she be --?"

"Do you know their names?"

"Otto, Ernst, and Jakob, but --"

"Say no more." Her pale, slim hands curled into fists, crumpling the scraps of paper within them.

"But *will* she be all right?" begged Tess, kneeling by Betje.

"In time, she will be," the chandleress said. "Once the shock has passed."

"Would he have … hurt her? Whichever one --?"

"Yes. He would have killed her, just as he's killed so many others."

Both girls swayed in horror, feeling their blood run like ice.

"We ..." Annika began, voice trembling in a mouse-squeak. "We must do something, tell someone … Uncle Pietr, or a magistrate --"

The chandleress shook her head. "No. Do nothing, tell no one. Except, perhaps, for your Old Mag. She will understand and keep the secret. The less you know, the better."

"But what about –?"

Lines of sudden cold blue light flashed between her pale knuckles. Wisps of white smoke wafted up. As she opened her fingers again, a fine ash-powder drifted to the floorboards. She smiled.

"Leave that to me," she said.

By this light, this candle's light
Now show me fair and true
What waits?
What fates?
What secrets hide?
What do I wish I knew?

The Devil's Spindle

By Scott J Laurange

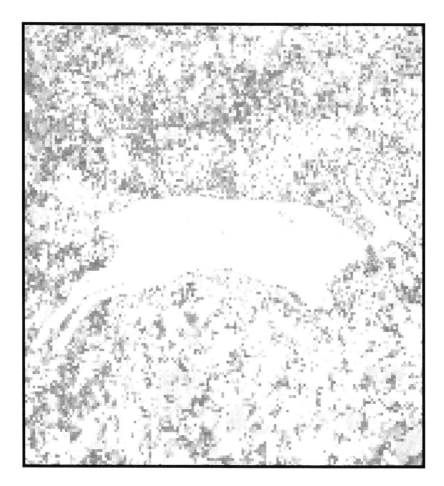

$\mathbf{H}$arvest time had risen ripe and full, and the sweet scent of apples hung heavy in the autumn air. The moon was plump, large in the crisp night sky, great and orange as it settled low on the horizon. Looking across the hay-filled field to the dense tree line on the far side, he knew it would be moments before the crows would take flight. They would be settled into the hay, awaiting their necessary moment of departure, presaging, as they always did, the events to follow. They would fly; he would cross the field toward the pines; the dead deer would lay curled in the hay off to his right side; and then all Hell would descend upon him. It happened every night this way—he could not escape the inevitable.

Crispin had been dreaming this night for weeks. The old man's tale had cemented the images in the young man's mind, made them real. But not so real as now, as he stood in the whispering breeze. Nature's dark secrets beckoned; Crispin had reached his destination. He'd trekked nine hundred miles in a beat up Dodge Dart from Beaufort, South Carolina, to the back woods of the Hudson Valley to spend months exploring the towns and the wilds of the land nestled about the Hudson River, the lumpy, sleeping giant of the Catskills always looming in the distance. He'd soaked in the atmosphere of the land, but more importantly, he'd been collecting tales. Crispin fancied himself something of a connoisseur of legends and folklore, sampling them for nose and body, ever in search of the enigmatic, fabled rarest of vintages—the tale that did not merely live in words and imaginations, but that walked the earth and could be experienced.

He'd begun with the obvious, the famous. He spent weeks in the area around that notorious widening of the Hudson, the Tappan Zee. He sat one whole full-mooned night at the tree line near the base of Hook Mountain, letting the haunted sounds of the wind and water wash over him. He sought the white lady, and Captain Vanderdecken, and the well of forgotten souls. And of course, he visited the Hollow, itself. Beautiful land—both landscape, and architecture. He could see why Washington Irving had loved it so, had been so willing to set his child in such geography. It was precariously balanced between proper civilisation and the dark wilds of the country surrounding it. In its very structures and shapes, it was a living battle between the desire for culture and community, and the unkempt and dangerous chaos of the past. He'd slept in the haunted buildings in town; he'd slept in the cemetery (awaking once from a terrible dream in which the dewy grass enfolded his body and pulled him down into the dirt—he could still taste the bitterness of the earth in his mouth when he startled awake); he'd slept in the forests. He'd been on the tours, listened to the tales, and even followed the trail of Ichabod's supposed flight from the fiendish Horseman. But the more he dug, the more he felt like he was trapped in some kind of theme park version of the true past. The town was trying too hard. It didn't have a yarn to spin, so much as it had a story to sell. Crispin needed more; his quest demanded it.

It was the toothless old woman outside the gift shop who sent him northward to find the old man with the right tale. She was Iroquois, possibly Mohawk—he'd not asked, as it had seemed an uncouth question—and blind in one eye, the other masked by a cataract. She gummed her way through her words, but seemed to know Crispin's quest on sight; recognized the obsession in his eye, the haunted shadow looming just behind him.

"Go north, my child," she'd rasped. "Soak up the land and seek the Children's Corner. You'll find the end you want there." He questioned her, but having said her piece, she acknowledged his presence no longer.

Northward he went, all along the Taconic, collecting more tales, more folklore, scrawling them in his frayed and tattered notebook.

Campfires and abandoned buildings became his home, his constant haunts as he soaked up the history and death-filled mythos of New England. He'd grown up with the ghosts of Beaufort's marshes, amidst the South's sense of pervasive death—that mournful, lost quality to the land and air and people that smacked of inheritance gone sour. Something had died in the South, and its mouldering corpse went ever marching on. But here, in the North, the darkness was alive, creaking and skittering and loping and gibbering through the land, hostile and deadly. The perimeter of light from every campfire he'd sat at in recent weeks was at best a weak barrier against what skulked in the darkness. The tales told ranged from barely credible to outrageous, but whatever was beyond that dim fire's light was real, and it made the tales real.

He spent one harrowing night alone on Bannerman's Island in the castle Frank Bannerman had built there, the wind rustling and moaning while the harvest moon hid behind the mountain of the island, and of those that lay beyond the river's water, so that whatever crept underneath the rock could have full sway and haunt those who would dare speak into the darkness. The excursion had nearly achieved what he was looking for—he felt the weight and life and power in the place—the feeling of the air compressing all around him. Something rising out of the earth, scraping at the ruined and burned stones in the husk of the castle. He thought of Irving once more, and the goblins thought to haunt the island. He was certain once that something had brushed his leg, but by the time he looked, there was nothing. He edged closer to his fire. Later, just as he was drifting off into an exhausted doze, a hideous wailing filled the air. He startled awake and grabbed for a large branch he had set just into the fire for a makeshift torch. He grabbed wrong in his haste and burned his hand. Once he managed to lift it, he caught sight of movement on the edge of a crumbling wall. He thrust the burning branch up high and spotted a loon. It stared at him impassively, then fluttered off into the dark. He slept no more, and the rest of the night was calm and uneventful.

As he travelled northward, he felt himself traveling also backward in time. It was no longer just the setting he sought, but the source. Sleepy Hollow was the result of a man's fantastical distillation of true legend and superstitious belief. It wasn't enough for Crispin; he needed the real thing—he needed to explore where the story came from. Many places claimed to be the true Sleepy Hollow; with the best of the stories, it was inevitable. The place with the name had earned that right because the details Irving had given corroborated it. But true places of legend are less certain, less plottable, less grounded in the cardinal directions. And the details of the tales he collected were anything but clear, direct, or grounded. Whether it be those directly related to Irving's story, or those rooted in other local legends (the nameless specters, the enigmatic and pervasive Green Ghost, or even Bigfoot sightings), they felt more authentic than those of Sleepy Hollow in the books.

Crispin thought it was *because* the details were so fleeting that he believed the tales. It was like hearing the crunch of leaves out in the woods. Probably a raccoon, or a deer (he thought again, now, of the dead one assuredly lying several feet away on his right), but because it was indistinct, and momentary, it could be *anything*. The smell of the air, the dead quality of the light, the deep, inscrutable thickness of the darkness beyond that light, the chill rising from the ground, the canopy of branches blocking out the night sky—all became pieces of reality behind the tales. A night like this said anything was possible.

And yet, with these many nights holding his imagination prisoner, none of those tales had been so convincing as the ones he'd listened to in the back of that candy shop.

This town, the Children's Corner—as the old woman had called it—the source of many of Irving's details, the place where he wrote a goodly chunk of the story, itself, was possessed of a deeper resonance, a sense of Lovecraft's cosmic otherness, a hint at the dark underbelly of America.

Crispin hadn't missed the irony in the candy shop. Out front, for the townsfolk and the tourists seeking "colonial heritage" in a village steeped in historical buildings and landmarks and, most importantly, true history, itself (for isn't history *really* to be found not as much in the mortar and brick but rather in the legends and the blood of the people who carried them through time?), the store presented an eye-pleasing masquerade of candy and toys and baubles and bric-a-brac. Striped candy sticks in myriad flavours—ten cents apiece; twelve for a buck. Kites and spools of kite string. Balsa wood airplanes. Candles. Locally woven blankets (some actually Iroquois—mostly Mohawk—some faux). Iron-worked figures. Indian beads. Useless porcelain figurines. The omnipresent glass unicorns. Every town has such a store—the eternal haunts of summer's children.

But behind the curtain, in the back rooms of these stores, sit the ancients, the elders. Every town has these, too. The old men who remember everything, who remember the past like it was playing out even now, who somehow seem to remember even before their own time. Anyone who disbelieves history to be a living, conscious thing need only sit and chat with these men. They don't dilute history, and they don't speak with bias. They speak of the darknesses of our past, of the land that has reared us, and they make us *believe* in them.

As he stood in the field now, in the present, dusk finally dying into night, Crispin smiled and shuddered simultaneously.

He had spent several afternoons in that backroom, listening to tales, waiting for the right one. The old timers had shared many with him. Some, he knew already. They were the "published" tales, the ones everyone knew—the kind he'd grown up on, reading by flashlight in a tent in the backyard or listening to, wide-eyed, as his grandpa's friends passed them back and forth over beers on a summer's eve—the ones told so many times they barely had any strength left to instill fear.

Some supported stories he'd heard on his journey, a mix of history and legend. They tied into Irving's tale—not the words on the page, but the ones behind those words. They told of the schoolteacher Jesse Merwin, friend of Irving, buried with his wife, Jane, not in the local cemetery as history claimed, but on his farm near the lake that would later be named for him. Crispin even hiked out there one day to see the gravestones which lay at the bottom of the old house's front steps. He could feel something in the autumn air—a presence or unseen observer—and a thrill shot up his spine. The old men spoke of many unexplained hauntings along that road. Nothing so sinister as a headless Hessian, but strange events, whispered voices, and missing persons aplenty. If the area outside Tarrytown were the skin of the legend, this place and these stories were the rotting heart at the core of it.

Beyond Irving, there were more tales, ones new to Crispin, and equally entrancing. They carried the familiar tropes, of course—wailing, lost loves returned from the grave; strange, lurking beasties; inexplicable occurrences and disappearances—but the details were new and different. There was a recent murder/ suicide on that road where Merwin had lived, and it had spawned all sorts of local rumours about geists, or ghouls, or psychic control. There were trees that became gaping maws straight to hell and which only opened under a new moon. There were winding roads that might change direction on the unsuspecting traveller, taking him to a land not of this plane. The number of vanished motorists in this part of the world was astonishingly high. There was the mysterious and enigmatic

Devil's Spindle, a stone totem of some sort, hidden in the woods. Most shied away from the details regarding that one. And there was the Lapwerk Man, a jumble of scarecrow bits and actual corpsely flesh. He could appear in your apple orchard or pumpkin patch or the side of the road or your fruit cellar. He was always looking for more parts to sew into his body.

Still, these were not the story he was looking for. These haunts could hail from anywhere, any when. But Crispin was on a hunt, a quest, a maddening search—a driving need to discover something specific, something "other" that defied reason and explanation. Something to chill his bones, to enmesh them with the ephemeral smell of history. He needed a living tale, one people still feared.

It wasn't the kind of tale people parted with willingly. Not the sane ones, at least. Fear is not as wild as people think—it's quite reasonable, actually. For it's fear that teaches people what to run and hide from, what deserves their respect, what should be held in silence. We do not speak the names of things we fear.

But after enough time, Crispin pried it out of the old men, and they told him.

It was Jim Haskell who told the story, though several others added a detail here and there. Jim was about eighty, hair white as Christmas and his face so wrinkled you had to guess which lines his eyes were hiding in. The perfect ambassador to an outsider like Crispin. He knew the land like no one else, and his voice evoked both gravel and honey—the natural voice for a tale of New England's spirits.

Charlie Van Allen had just finished spinning a ghost yarn (he told the same one every day and they all let him—it was one of the few things Charlie still did well), when Jim slowly stood and hobbled to the cabinet in the minuscule kitchenette. Crispin felt as though the curtains had just gone up and the performance had begun, as if the last week had been a mere rehearsal to the real deal. Jim, now fully in costume, brought back a fifth of whiskey and two glasses. After numberless cups of decaf Sanka, Crispin knew he'd *finally* found his way into the castle of the Fisher King and was angled at last toward his journey's grail. Jim sat, seemed to consider a goodly while, then spun the cap off the whiskey with his thumb and poured. He slid one glass across to Crispin, stared into his own several moments before downing half in a gulp, then began the tale. He offered no explanation, no disclaimer, no preface. He just spoke.

"They say there's an infection in the land north of here. Right up them hills, back amongst the trees. Ain't sure if it's ghosts or demons or living beasties. No one is. But *something's* gotten into the land and rotted it. Oh, not so's you can see any physical sign of it. The trees are as dense and live as ever. They change with the seasons as they're supposed to, or remain ever green as their name suggests. The critters scurry just like they ought. The wind cries its laments or sighs like the creaking straw in a scarecrow's head like it always does in the depths of autumn. Yet you can feel something ain't right. The air's heavier. The hay don't lay right. The leaves shiver with fear, not with the wind. And animals die for no reason."

Jim paused to take a sip from his whiskey, then sat thoughtfully for several more moments before continuing, less the philosopher now and more the tale spinner. And he told it well—the hook was laid with the first words, laden with colloquial charm and magic, and his manner dangled and pulled until it was firmly snared in Crispin's mind. To really make his catch, his brow furrowed slightly, as if the story pained him to tell—or he questioned the wisdom of telling it to this particular audience.

He said, "I was twelve the year I came closest to what's out there. I was cutting across some backyards and wild acreage to get home afore dark and dinnertime. You didn't want to upset the matriarchal sense of order—dinner was at the time designated, and you didn't miss it on your life. If that meant a detour through some circle of Hell or another, or a tad bit of trespassing, you took the risk. Because mom's disapproving eye was worse. Leastways so I thought.

"The deer wasn't quite dead when I near tripped over it. If it hadn't been for the mound of shale pushing its way up out'n the earth, I would have landed face first in the animal's gore. The added height of the rock let me catch a glimpse and leap at the last second to land in the tall grass on the other side of it. And I stared into its not-quite-dead-but-lunatic eyes, and lost the hunger for mom's roast chicken. Its neck had been twisted around backward, and the animal had been disemboweled. This was no hunter's trophy, no accident victim, the nearest road being miles away on the other side of murky ponds and dense woods. This was deliberate maiming. I remember staring into the black, dying eyes of the deer; I remember its jaws parted to reveal its tongue protruding between its teeth, shuddering as if lapping at non-existent *aqua vitae*."

Something gnawed at the back of Crispin's mind about Jim's manner in the telling of the story. He felt (but could not put proper words to the feeling) that Jim spoke as if he were two people, two separate characters. It may just have been that he wasn't fully in control of his story voice, but for the briefest moment, Crispin suspected Jim was a mask concealing a very different persona. He might have considered this nothing more than a show, but then, the story beckoned, and enticed, and cajoled and his imagination begged for more, following it like a lost puppy. The voice, whether refined wordsmith or local tale spinner, got him just the same.

"I remember the opening in her belly," Jim continued, looking downward and to the left as if trying to summon that memory, "which glistened in the waning light, and how I could tell it wasn't cut, but punched or ripped open. And I remember the way her front hoof lay across the other, a peaceful aspect to an otherwise horrible scene of violence (not that I thought about it as such at the time). Finally, I remember the shudder that ran through it as its last breath huffed out and its heart, which I'd felt thudding behind my eyes, came to a stop.

"My senses returned to me as the thought of *bear* entered my mind. I glanced all round me as I scooted on my backside away from the deer until I could gain my feet, and then I ran like holy Hell."

Jim paused long enough for another sip of whiskey (Crispin had already refilled his glass twice) before jumping right back into his tale. He knew he held his audience captive and wasn't the sort of storyteller to play coy. Cat and mouse was just cruel; a proper tale spinner cornered his prey, then went straight for heart, mind, and soul until all were caught in a silver-lined web.

"Course, it wasn't until I hit the tree line that I realised I was running the wrong way. And what do you do at that point? You're twelve, ascared out'n your wits, and you've got two choices—run *back* toward the death you just gazed into (and like as much the *source* of that death), or delve into the deep of the woods right as the last of the daylight was about to wink out, and pray you made it out the other side. That's the kind of choice that ain't."

Crispin nodded his assent to this statement as if it needed his stamp of approval.

"It was then that I saw a light wink on somewhere in the woods. Wasn't fireflies—I knew that. Had a sense of fire to it, but I could tell it wasn't campfire and yet it didn't move like a torch bore by a person either. There was a sense of … of something organic to it. Like the fire was alive, but also *held* by something alive. And it wasn't just my eyes at work, mind you. There was a chittering—not like squirrels or anything else natural to them woods—something that had meaning behind it. Chittering, but in intelligent language.

"There's about one thing in this world that'll quash fear *and* self-preservation right quick and at the same time: curiosity. It got its hooks into me, and I *had* to know what I was seeing. I wish to this very day I'd made good on that, but I still don't know what I saw. I'll tell it, but I'll be damned if I can offer an explanation. Maybe you'll get that when you seek it; I know you will' 'cause it's why you're here. I won't try to talk you out of it—I seen that look before. It's a *hunger*, it is—but I will say I wish you wouldn't. It can't end well, son."

Crispin swallowed hard at that. Jim had spoken with such sorrow in his voice, as if the younger man was already lost. For the briefest of moments, he almost reconsidered his quest. But in the end, he knew he must seek and find, no matter the cost. The warning Jim had offered was expected; in fact, Crispin would have felt cheated had it not been made. He drained another glass of whiskey, then bade Jim to continue with a nod.

"The grounds sloped down as I made my way deeper into the woods," he said. "It wasn't much of a grade at all, but I had the distinct sense of leaving this world as I walked. By this time, it was full dark. The thick tree cover should have blotted out most of the moonlight and kept my vision to a nightmarish nothing, but the strange moving fire ahead of me let me see a great deal. I was grateful for that—I'd have had a few pretty bad spills otherwise. The air had growed mighty close, too, as I got further in. Felt like I was moving *against* something—and *it* was winning. I could feel my leg muscles straining. But on I went, fool that I was. I think we all go on, when we get that far down the path.

"Then I found it. The Devil's Spindle. Huge, cylindrical rock, pointing up toward the heavens like a rude gesture. Had to be fifteen or twenty feet high at its needle sharp point, and at its base, just above where the stone totem had thrust violently out'n the earth, was a wide, disc-like platform. Devil's Spindle—looking for all the world like it was just waiting to weave some yarn, or maybe the fated threads of a young boy's death. People always talked of it in hushed tones, but no one ever dared claim to have seen it. And here it was, towering above me like a threat. And like a taunt."

He paused, seeming almost wistful. Finally, he continued. "I took the bait, and headed deeper into the woods." A strange light gleamed in the old man's eyes, but Crispin could not match an emotion to it.

"Of a sudden," Jim said, "I broke out of the trees onto the edge of a clearing. I stopped dead, realising how exposed I was, then, as smoothly as I could manage, withdrew back into the trees. Looking out to the centre of the field—a good five hundred feet off—flames danced. Not like they do in a cozy fireplace, but like something living. They *danced*. It was rhythmic; hell, it was *sensual*. I can't say as I fully understood what that meant at the time, but my guts kenned it nonetheless. There were distinct, individual flames, but they moved as one, and gave the impression of a great writhing snake made of flame, circling around and around something I could not make out. Ever so often, I caught a glimpse of some small, lithe figure of shadow beneath, or maybe even within the flames. Something carrying the fire, or emanating it. But they moved as one, with perfection and seductive grace.

"The whole scene was mesmerizing—and I wanted to *join*. I came within a breath of leaping from my spot in the trees and darting across the field to take my place in the dance. And then the baby's cry went up into the still night air. Remembering the dead deer, I thought for a moment it could be a fawn. Same creepy child cry. But then it cried again, and the voice hitched just a bit the way only a human baby's does when it's cold and hungry and ascared."

Jim paused and downed the rest of his whiskey, then poured another glass and swallowed half of it. Crispin passed him a significant look that involved much raised eyebrows and suggested he'd best continue the tale or suffer bodily harm. The young man was, clearly, bitten by that worst of bugs: belief.

"Well," Jim said, "what do you think I did? I'm no hero—and I was a kid, myself. I rabbited, fast as can be. Managed to make it home without dying or wetting myself. Count that as a win to this day."

For the first time since the story began, Crispin spoke, his voice thick from the whiskey. "Did you find out what it was? I mean, you must have *wanted* to know."

Jim smirked, one corner of his mouth stretched up in bitter irony. "Does anyone ever figure these things out, son? Satanists, other cultists *du jour*, spectral reoccurrence of some ancient injun rite—hell, I can guess all day. Of course I wanted to know, but that fear wasn't something I could ever get around. Those who seek to know too much don't come back. That's always the way, innit? When we're done here, I expect this'll be the last I see you, too. No, son, I have no idea what it was, nor do I care to. But I can tell you it's regular as the Devil, and the signs are always the same. It's feeding something, and that something doesn't like to go hungry." He paused, registering the eagerness in Crispin's eyes. Then he sighed, came to a decision, and stood with a slight shake of his head. "I'm done here, son. Need to get home 'fore my gal decides she's a widow and sells off all my stuff. Woman has a bit of Old Scratch in her when she doesn't get her way. I've warned you all I can, I know that. Last thing I can do is beg. Don't put yourself on that menu—no amount of knowledge is worth it."

And with that, he turned and forced his tired legs out the door.

And the warning was heeded as much as the old man expected.

Two more weeks Crispin waited while the moon crept toward the right phase, and the crows and deer and strange occurrences in the woods—all the eerie details of Jim's tale—haunted his dreams. Sometimes, they appeared as literal interpretations of the old man's account; sometimes they morphed into huge, shadowy, misshapen things that writhed across the tips of the tall grass to consume him in darkness.

Then they began to haunt his waking life as well. He saw them, often only for a moment, on the tops of buildings or flagpoles or fences or the grassy square as he walked along the town centre of the Children's Corner. And then they appeared on window sills or the top of the bathroom stall or above his B&B room's chamber door—Poe-esque all the way. And finally, he had to admit the cosmos was assertively thrusting an omen upon him. It wasn't what he was accustomed to. In the South, a crow (or sparrow or owl—any psychopomp would do, really) might dive bomb your iced tea as you sat some evening on the porch, or beat itself senseless (or dead) against the kitchen window. Apparently, in New England, the omens stalked you, organized and methodical until you were paranoid enough to heed the warning.

It *almost* worked. Almost. At last the harvest moon rose, and now Crispin stood in the field of dead grass; he watched the crows rise into the waning light. They did not lift in fear, but out of purpose. Like an obligation. Like a condemnation.

A short moment later, the field and sky were clear of all but the descending darkness and glow of the full September moon. Out in the distance he spied a place where the grass was broken and flattened in a rough circle. It was where the deer would lay.

He walked toward it, drawn by inevitability, then parted the tall grass and knelt by the carcass. He'd expected dead. Despite old Jim's tale, he hadn't bargained on dissected. It wasn't clinical—there was no technique or skill. No human hand had cut open the deer; neither professional nor novice would leave such jagged, raw rips in the flesh. Yet, there *was* a surgical quality to the opening in the carcass's belly. There was intent, and that purpose was to leave the vitals undamaged, even if the way *to* the vitals was haphazard and messy. Of course, Crispin could only assume the intention was to keep the vitals sound and safe—they were no longer present, so he had to gather that the *wanting* of them was enough to secure their integrity. Crispin was no expert on a deer's innards, but even he could tell that heart, and lungs, and stomach and more were gone, removed. He stared into the open cavity of that deer, hide and flesh torn back and hanging open like a cat-shredded curtain, and wondered if he should consider this as one last portent to heed Jim's warning. Portents were, historically speaking, read in animals' entrails. The entrails in question were missing, but the effect was the same. This was a blaring message, a resounding gong, a noise to waken him from the sleep that had thickened his mind since embarking on this trek. Oh, but his imagination—now *that* was prophet, soothsayer, and snake oil man—its interpretation of the deer charmed and lulled him back to slumber. His imagination proclaimed the tinder here in the mangled flesh to promise blazing flames further on the journey.

Crispin stood in the high grass. And the elation of the hunt, the search, the quest filled his heart and his guts. He turned to face the woods that old Jim Haskell had fled to without his wits. And he smiled, and walked into the dark forest, leaving the dull orange glow of the moon behind.

Crispin had spent plenty of time traveling and camping in the "approved" forests over the last weeks. Those were mapped, had trails, were of civilization. But what he now entered—this was the true wilderness, untamed and inscrutable. He had expected . . . well, woods. Woods are woods, right? From the first crunch of leaves beneath his step, from the first scent of pine and moss and bark and nettles and animal, from the first sense of pressure all around him—of trees and life and thick air and something *other* and indefinable—Crispin knew he was in a strange new world. The ghosts of centuries were here. The presence of nature's life and the past's death hung in the air like fog—intangible, but thick and smothering. He had often ruminated over the history in people's blood; he'd never before felt and smelled and tasted it in the air, brushing the pores of his skin, tickling his nose, whispering in his ears, pleading with his lips for passage to his lungs and life. This forest was alive, and dead, and undead, and it frightened Crispin on a level so deep and basic in his humanity that he near lost all sense of self and self-preservation. He wanted to cry, laugh, run, and die. Simultaneously. He wanted to scream, and to sing. He wanted to lie down and pull the earth about himself like a shroud, to kneel and worship the land. He wanted this moment to be his dreams and his nightmares, to last, *and* to be his last. If one can have a praise-God-Almighty-alleluia conversion to the dark side of nature, then this was it for Crispin.

He felt the tears coursing down his cheeks, and willed his legs to move him forward.

The firelight Jim had spoken of had yet to show itself, and since the trees' canopy blocked out most of the moonlight, the going was slow. Crispin had brought no flashlight. His quest was sacred, and any artificial illumination would violate that sanctity. So he groped through the trees, taking slow steps through the underbrush, stumbling on roots and rocks and who knows what else (he tried not to think about that thing that both crunched and squelched as his knee came down hard upon it), falling in leaf-mould and moss and mud, then picking himself up and carrying on.

The cities have forgotten about darkness, about its density, about what it feels like to become lost in it (which is ironic, since they've conjured a wholly different manner of darkness all their own). Those who have lived with sight and then lost it know some of the feeling. But it's much more despairing when you know your sight still *works*, and yet can discern nothing. It is claustrophobia for the eyes, and the clawing frenzy creeps upon you just as sure.

Yet Crispin pushed forward, despite butting heads several times with trees and nearly impaling an eye on a low-hanging and sharply pointed branch. He moved on instinct, feeling the dark like a warm sponge soaking up his senses, pulling him to it. The night seemed to want him, and he it. His feet, slavish, followed the dark's draw without his mind's acquiescence.

And he soon noticed a differentiation in the dark. There were outlines where once had been nothing. He could see motion, if not distinct forms. And he realized it was reflected light that offered him this glimpse. Ten or twenty easier steps later, and brightness flared in the near distance. Just a glow, but more intense than anything he'd seen since the sun had taken its final dip below the horizon. And then he saw it clearly—the brief burst of flame Jim had described. It appeared on the side of a tree, illuminating the bark and branches and leaves in stark contrast to the pervading dark, contracted into a brighter, more intense spot—a sort of mini-sun prior to bursting forth in supernova—then bounded forth, dissipating quickly into the darkness, only to re-ignite on the side of another tree several yards ahead in the forest. Though the flame was momentary, its rebounding from tree to tree did, as Jim had said, give the impression of a body or figure within, or possibly holding the flame. It was humanoid, but shrunken, perhaps withered or homuncular.

Crispin ran through his mental catalogue of folklore, and settled on goblins or imps as the likeliest match. He shivered with excitement.

As he followed along, he heard the chittering Jim had spoken of. It was a wry, mocking sort of noise. Conversational, yet manic; inhuman, yet intelligible. If he hadn't already used up his get-out-of-jail-free cards, this was certainly the last one available. The creepy, tainted quality of the noise dug deeply under Crispin's skin and warned him to flee for his life, if not for his sanity, his soul.

He couldn't listen. The fire, the quest, had him in thrall.

The flame got ahead of him, but he followed it until a sinister tower of shadow brought him up short. The Devil's Spindle.

It was obscene, a sharp and angry curse thrust upward into the night. At a glance, it appeared to be of the same shale that was so prevalent in the region, but as he moved in closer, he thought it might be obsidian, which made little sense here in New England. He reached out to it, hesitant, and finally willed his fingers to run across the surface. He felt carvings, sigils of some sort all along the rock—unintelligible and alien. The Spindle loomed above him, silent and threatening, and he thought for a moment to turn back. He pulled his hand away, and walked on.

Soon, he reached the edge of the clearing. He stopped at the border and took cover behind the last of the trees.

Though he'd chased a single flame through the dark wood, many now streamed out across the field to coalesce in the centre and begin rhythmic undulations in a hectic ring-around-the-rosey.

Crispin could not wait in the wings as Jim had. He needed not just to see some strange phenomenon, possibly hear suggestive sounds. He needed to witness the truth of the event. Hunched, he crept from the trees and made his way across the field. He realised, but did not stop to consider, that the grass here should have been high like the autumn grass where the deer had lain dead, but was instead cut low. Cut, not merely short in growth. He thought, but did not internalize, that this took intention and planning. He felt, but did not heed, the shivering in the marrow of his bones, which pled with him to flee.

He could feel the quick thump of his heart begin in his chest and echo in his ears, could hear the air rushing in and out of his lungs (the sound dampened somewhat and made hollow by that echoed thumping), could see that breath pluming before him in the steadily chilling, moonlit night air. He closed the distance as fast as he dared, though stealth seemed a darned silly endeavour with no concealment of any kind between the shelter of trees he'd left behind and the circle of dancing flames he advanced toward.

And then he stopped. Twenty-five feet to go, maybe thirty. You always hear about blood running cold. Metaphorical, of course—it can't run cold lest you're dead, and if you're dead it isn't running, now is it? But Crispin stood still as a man who *was* dead already, and he certainly felt as if ice slicked the inside of his veins, like of a sudden, someone had hooked him up to an IV of freon. But then, whether a story led you there or not, even a tale you believed in your gut, the cry of a baby—terrified, cold, and alone—will get the same result; the blood runs cold, every time. Crispin had, of course, suspected that the twelve-year old mind of Jim Haskell had been playing tricks, that fright had turned the sounds of nature into something human. Crispin had believed, yet had not believed. He had wanted a *story*, a tale, a legend, not Truth. Had he truly believed in his heart of hearts, he might have gotten a different story altogether. In the end, he got what he wanted. He got to be part of the story.

Yes, his blood may have run cold, but his legs kept him moving after that initial shock. And then the whole scene showed plain before him.

Low rounded stones were spaced around a stone table, upon which squalled a newborn babe. Within the perimeter of the stone circle danced misshapen creatures holding (though not encased within, as had seemed in the forest) simple flaming torches. And Crispin recognized them for both who and what they were.

When Man fell, he fell to gain the knowledge of both good and evil. This entails the kind of complexity that ain't right to speak of here, but simply, it was a double-edged blade—man could *act* in both manners, and he could also know them when he saw them. This was the first time

Crispin had seen evil's true face, and he knew it on sight. Looking on the maskless demonic will do that—allow honesty of interpretation, I mean. And yet, as with any lie, there's always a bit of truth in the mask. And so, in looking at those dancing with flame around that babe, Crispin could see the truth that had reflected in the lies, in the masks, in the *story*. He saw Charlie Van Allen, and old Ned Hasbrouck, and Amos De Witt, and Linus Ostrander, and Mildred Hagen (whose poor husband had met with a terrible end at the hands of a scoundrel scientist in the twenties), and Abe Jansen, and Stan Kieslowski, among others of the elders. And, of course, he saw me (or what he thought of as Jim Haskell as that was the story he wanted to see) and your grandma, standing over your poor, cold, crying form.

The last thing Crispin saw (in his sane mind at least, though there wasn't much left of it by now), was you tearing that ridiculous mask from your beautiful, soot-colored face and smiling up at the autumn moon with your real eyes for the first time.

The world never really took much notice of that man, Crispin, and he wasn't missed when he vanished. But he was vital to you, my boy. He was your first human, and his insatiable need to know the tale's end was a veritable (and movable, as it turns out, since he was quite the sprinter, even if he was out of his right mind) feast for your eyes, and for everything else.

We don't get into this world very easily, my boy, but we do have a legacy to uphold.

Remember, it's not just how you tell the tale, but *who* you tell it to. A story is useless without a believer. And Crispin believed like few before him have, and few others ever will. But here in New England, in the heart of the Hudson Valley, we make our own legends.

Remember—salvation is in the warning all tales *must* provide. The trick—*our* trick—is in getting them to *ignore* the warning.

Now, boy, run along, and tell your grandma I'm just going to finish this here Sanka. Wouldn't want her to think I've been exorcised. She'd sell all my stuff in a heartbeat, the devil-woman.

PASSING THROUGH

By James C. Simpson

It was late in the evening, and the clock was ticking ever closer to the witching hour, when the superstitious claimed all sorts of evils would populate the earth, the dead would rise from their graves, and the devil would cause all manner of mischief. The few men who had gathered in the tavern near the outskirts of Sleepy Hollow, New York, were accustomed to such tales of terror. Mostly because they were often the ones telling them.

Sleepy Hollow was, of course, a rather infamous spot for those romantically inclined to consider stories of ghosts and goblins to be real. The entire region had a certain magic lingering over it. Since childhood, the men in the tavern had spent countless evenings with the many local legends of the region, many of which were well known even to outsiders. The famous Autumn ride of the Headless Horseman through the woods was a favorite tale of the locals, and the men enjoyed retelling it, particularly to gullible travelers. The infamous decapitated ghost was just one of many such specters and ghouls haunting the region. Other stories revolved around witches conducting peculiar rituals long since abandoned in the New World, bloodsucking creatures from beyond the grave, and malevolent spirits seeking vengeance on the living.

"We've heard all these before," Mr. Marley noted to Nathaniel Christian, the young man who was in the process of giving one of his animated oratories. "Surely, you must know some new ones, my young friend." Marley motioned to the young man with a wave of his hand, prodding the storyteller to reach further within for inspiration.

Nathaniel was a tad bit embarrassed and his face blushed, but he remedied the situation by downing another shot of brandy. Two others were gathered around the roaring fireplace with Nathaniel and Mr. Marley. One, Mr. Barlowe, was middle-aged while the other, Abraham, was closer in age to Nathaniel. They all came from different backgrounds: rich and poor, student and lawyer. Yet joined by a shared love for all things macabre.

Each of them took turns telling their stories, but Nathaniel was the undisputed favorite, delivering each yarn with such ghoulish relish the men would pester him for a tale each time they met. He had told so many at this point he had nearly exhausted the local legends and was reduced to spinning a new take on the already familiar, such as the one about the bride locked in a box in the attic on her wedding day, or the one about the escaped criminal with a hook for a hand.

Urged on by his fellows, the young man was pondering what yarn to spin when a sudden burst of thunder clapped in the distance. It was as if he was receiving a spark of inspiration. He leaped from his comfortable chair, almost spilling his drink, and exclaimed that he did, indeed, have a new story to tell.

"You may be familiar with a character in the story," he cautioned, "but I doubt you are aware of its connection to our haunted region." Calm and confident in his choice, Nathaniel sat back down.

"It's difficult to be surprised these days!" Abraham jested to his friend, who agreed with a silent nod.

"This is a peculiarly charmed region when it comes to the supernatural and the fantastic, I must admit," agreed Nathaniel. "That's why this next story may surprise you. It was told to me by my grandfather and took place many years ago, shortly after our revolution and not far from our most famous local tale." Nathaniel smiled at his friends, and the men returned the gesture, each raising a glass in silent acknowledgement of Irving's masterpiece. Outside the window, a crack of lighting provided the perfect setup for a tale of terror.

"Many strange things lurked in this corner of the globe during that desperate time. We were a young nation, having narrowly won our independence. The world was a savage place, and most of what we now consider civilization was still a vast wilderness. My grandfather had returned home from the conflict a weary yet satisfied man. He believed he had fought for a just cause but had known much in the way of hardship and terror. Now that the cannons had stopped firing and there was no longer any soldiering to be done, he took residence in his old home where he would study his books and papers. My grandfather was a very learned man and was known as something of a scholar. He was well versed on most subjects and particularly on the new sciences. He marveled at Mr.

Franklin's discovery of electricity and understood its potential. Of course, he was not alone in that thinking, and he learned of how such power was harnessed. Europe was a hotbed of experimentation into this new frontier, and my grandfather read of the many strange and fantastic things men were doing with this new science. This is why he came to fear the stranger that passed through that late autumn day, so long ago."

Nathaniel stopped for a moment and took a sip from his brandy before asking the men if they had ever heard of a killer known as "The Bear Man."

They had indeed heard the story and acknowledged as such.

"I remember hearing of him in the lecture halls," the youngest man mentioned, his child-like face exuding a certain wide-eyed terror, coupled with a devilish sort of glee. "Our professor described him as a most violent man who was said to rend and tear his victims apart like a wild animal. He was said to have been as powerful as a bear, hence the nickname. Few claimed to have seen him, but those that did said he was as big as a giant and had the appearance of something horrifically dreadful. Almost as if he had been a denizen of the grave come back to life!" The young man cackled after giving this morbid description, the other men laughing along with him at the absurdity of the tale. Nathaniel, however, merely cracked the smallest of grins.

"Yes, I am familiar with the tale," said Nathanial, sighing and looking pensively out the window. "The version I heard from my grandfather, however, is a bit more detailed. You see, he met the Bear Man, himself. All those years ago."

The others were shocked at this revelation, and demanded to learn the identity of the long-lost, mysterious killer. They pleaded for Nathaniel to recount the sinister meeting between the legendary butcher and Nathaniel's grandfather, now long in his grave. He smiled for a brief moment, then began to cast his spell.

"My grandfather had returned from the war and settled peacefully in the home we know today, located on the outskirts of our community. He enjoyed the solitude, and after years of anguish and fear, such a simple life was preferable. He found himself immersed in the simple work of his homestead and his books--which he had neglected for far too long. He would occasionally encounter visitors at his home but they were usually the common assortment of hunters, trappers, and lost persons who had little business traveling unoccupied through the woods. Otherwise, he led a generally peaceful existence. Animals were hardly any nuisance, as bears and coyotes were usually chased away by a shotgun blast. I mention this because it had always perplexed me how the killings were often attributed to a bear, when we all know damn well no bear lives here that could have been responsible for the crimes described. My grandfather likely came to the same conclusion when he discovered the first victim in the late Autumn."

Nathaniel paused and reached for a glass of water, careful not to indulge in too much brandy. He needing a clear head and smooth tongue to continue the story.

"Where did he find the first victim?" Mr. Barlowe had known Nathaniel since he was a boy and had been an acquaintance of his late grandfather. However, he had never before heard of the old man's connection to this ancient crime.

"My grandfather was out patrolling the yards in the early morning with pipe, dog, and shotgun," continued Nathaniel. "He had been hoping for some game birds to present themselves, but was equally content to enjoy the peaceful hours before daylight. He was walking along a dirt path leading into the forest behind the homestead and hoping to find his favored place in front of a large rock that looked over the valley where he could watch the sunrise. Unfortunately, instead of the tranquility of the morning sun kissing the green grass and sparkling dew, he found the crumpled form of a man.

"My grandfather approached the body with some trepidation. The dog barked and growled, but would not approach the mangled corpse. It was indeed a terrible sight. My grandfather had seen much in the war, and knew all too well of how the body of a man could be corrupted and eviscerated, but he had never seen anything approaching this level of horror. The body was slumped like a child's forgotten doll, hunched over in an unnatural way, as if it lacked bones to support it. They were there in gruesome evidence, however, protruding from the broken skin of the unfortunate young man. His shattered remains were strewn about the stones, as if tossed about by a rabid hound. Near him were the smashed and broken remnants of a firearm, and from the scent of gunpowder in the air, he ascertained that it had been fired, perhaps multiple times. Clutched in the pale, stiff hand of the deceased was a dagger covered in blood of a purplish color. It appeared, to him at least, to be the blood of one long dead.

"Considering that no such puncture or stab wounds were found on the body, the dried blood on the blade could not belong to the victim. Point of fact, the body showed no signs that any weapon had been used upon it. Rather, the body had clearly been mauled and crushed to death by something of immense physical strength.

"Despite his worry that the proximity of the body to his cabin would make him a suspect, my grandfather notified the authorities, who came and carted the body back to town. Examiners were called in from New York City to inspect and dissect the remains, and all were astounded by the trauma and abuse that the body had taken. Some believed he had fallen, but this was ruled out as there was nothing nearby to have fallen from from. Nor could a fall explain the expression of absolute terror on the youth's face. His blood-filled eyes stared into space at something so utterly terrifying, my grandfather questioned whether it could have been the demonic visage of Satan himself.

"It was officially declared as a wild animal attack, though this was scoffed at by many-my grandfather included. Everyone knew there simply were no such animals in the area that could have done such ungodly damage. Of course, it was thought no man *living* could have caused such levels of carnage either, and so there were no probable suspects. Shortly thereafter, the perpetrator struck again, and that's when the name of the "Bear Man," was coined, for there had been a witness to the crime.

"It was not my grandfather who first saw this man, rather it was a near-vagrant by the name of Romney Talmadge, well known to frequent the local tavern at any given time of the day. That night, he was walking aimlessly about when he chose to ramble down a woodland path and seek shelter in an old hunting cabin. Along his way, however, he heard the high pitched scream of an attack. He at first assumed it to be a coyote bringing down a rabbit for a midnight meal--a sound which can be quite unsettling to the ear when heard. It wasn't until Talmadge came to a clearing and saw the figure of a man in the moonlight that he realized the scream was of human origin, caused by the stretching of one's vocal chords beyond any comfortable measure.

"It is a gruesome detail to be repeated, but repeat I must. Talmadge claimed to see the man lift his victim's man's head clean off, as easily as one would pick an apple from a tree. Talmadge gasped at the sight and let loose a scream of his own, causing the man to turn toward him and stand to his full height. He was taller than any human Talmadge had ever seen, more like an immense bear than a man. He wore a strange assemblage of furs, tattered and stitched together. And his face...his face was something not even Dante could have conceived! Upon seeing what he described as a visage of pure evil. Talmadge's feet found their step, and he ran faster than he'd ever set foot to path in his life."

"So how did your grandfather encounter the Bear Man?" asked a captivated Marley.

Nathaniel paused, frowning a moment, before continuing. "There were three murders in as many days, and the town and surrounding counties grew alarmed. A militia was formed, and men patrolled all hours of the night. The local gunsmith was swarmed with orders for higher caliber weapons, as many still suspected an animal of some great size, despite Talmadge's tale. Others spread rumors of an unnaturally large man roaming the forests in the dead of night, though no evidence could ever be found to support these sightings.

"My grandfather had procured a heavy bore rifle shortly after the war, sold to him by a trapper friend who had hunted buffalo in the great uncharted territories of the western frontier. He also kept on his person a horse pistol, which he had carried with him during his time in the military. He later admitted to me that it was fortunate my grandmother had not yet moved in, for he would have been in such a constant state of worry and fear for her safety, that it would likely have consumed him.

"Nearby the old home was an even older residence, long since abandoned. It had been constructed during the earliest days of colonization and had fallen to ill repair. The building was but a thatched roof with crumbling walls. Naturally, a derelict structure such as that spawned tales of hauntings by restless spirits. Of course, the old Dutch inhabitants who populated the area often thought every old building had a specter or demon lurking behind their decaying walls.

"It was perhaps foolish of my grandfather to be so foolhardy to remain alone in that vast wilderness, but he was a man who feared little, and he resolved to face and conquer any and all life threw at him. At least this is what he told himself. But when his dog ran off shortly after sunset and he heard the strange howling and scuffling coming from that abandoned place, he felt the gooseflesh creep up on him much as it had on the field of battle.

"He grabbed his rifle, powder horn, and lead balls and hurried through the forest, the moonlight guiding the way. It can be sure that curses uttered from his lips as he went after his errant hound who had dashed from the home at the most inopportune time. Grandfather hated traveling toward such a place as the old abandoned home in the dark, especially with a supposedly mad killer about, but he was armed and, as I described before, fearless. Making his way toward the clearing and the ruins of the old home, he noticed a light on the horizon. It appeared that *someone* had taken refuge within. At first he assumed it to be another lost hunter or possibly a member of one of the many search parties who were wont to track and hunt after this fiend, but a silence in the air made him reconsider. His dog had barked all the way to the old home, but now there was not even a whimper, nor could he hear any birds or night creatures around him. It was as if he were all alone and everything about him was dead. Except he did not feel completely alone, for he felt prying eyes surveying each step he took toward that crumbling facade.

"He tightened the grip on his rifle, made sure to bring back the hammer, and eased himself along the path leading to the house when he heard a crunching sound behind him. His feet stopped, and so did the sound behind him. His heart beat faster and his breathing became shallow as he tried to control himself and his imaginary fear, certain he was in no danger. Then he resumed his approach toward the home and heard the crunching behind him, now closer than before. That's when he noticed a looming shadow over the gravel of the path before him, hulking and towering over his like some monstrous monolith."

Nathaniel paused and looked over the spellbound faces of his audience. "When began this story, I made mention of my grandfather's interest in science and technology. He had read of all the advances being made around the world and marveled at the progress made in such a short time. This may not seem pertinent or relevant at the moment, but I remind you of this so that you may understand why my grandfather would have any inclination of the identity of what lurked behind him.

"He turned on his heels, holding his rifle at the hip, and faced something hulking in the shadows of the night, its back against the moon, face obscured by darkness. It was huge in stature and loomed like a great bear over him, but there could be no question that it was a man. Yes there was something misshapen about the frame of the creature. It walked on two legs, its clothing as described by the drunk--a peculiar mixture of hides and ragged cloth, dark and torn, with crude stitching to close the seams. It had long flowing black hair that swayed in the night breeze, and its hands hung from lanky arms and appeared to clutch and grasp of their own will--as if in remembrance of holding a warm throat.

"When his eyes adjusted to the darkness, my grandfather saw the face of this behemoth and gasped. It was not as he could have possibly ever imagined. The drunk and others that had glimpsed this being had not conceived of how terrible was its countenance. It was not merely the face of a corpse, but a mismatched myriad of stitching and fragments held together. The yellow skin was pulled tight across its large skull and its thin black lips smiled in an almost permanent grin. Its yellow, watery eyes formed a horrid contrast with its white sockets and expressed a fury that would not have been out of place in the pits of Hell.

"My grandfather could not believe his eyes. He stood, transfixed, and gawked at the awful face as the hands of the thing slowly reached out for him--the massive fingers yellowed and leathery, clutching and seeking his throat! Grandfather knew what stood before him. It was no ordinary man. It was not some daemon from the pit, nor a specter haunting the grounds. This was something of man's own creation. The description was much too close. He remembered the story told to him of the arrogant medical student from Switzerland who had supposedly cobbled together a body from charnel house fragments and pieces from the morgue, constructed a man, and brought him to life through some chemical or electrical means. It had escaped and was rumored to have terrorized the countrysides of Europe. Now, apparently, it was here in the New World, and in the process of snuffing out my grandfather's life.

Mr. Barlowe squirmed uncomfortably in his chair as Nathaniel came to the climax of his tale.

"My grandfather tried to lift his rifle, but the monster easily overcame him and dashed the weapon away from his grasp," continued Nathaniel. "My grandfather made a grab for the rifle but the monster took hold of his shirt with a single meaty paw and threw him back against the gravel. He landed in a heap, yet he had the presence of mind to quickly draw his hunting knife, with which he slashed at the creature. Infuriated, the beast made to dive atop my grandfather and crush the life from him when the dog attacked, leaping on the fearsome mockery of death. The beast distracted for a moment, my grandfather pulled out his heavy horse pistol and aimed it directly at the monster's head. As the creature flung the dog off his back--the faithful animal landing with a yelp and bouncing back to its feet--the old soldier clicked back the hammer and made clear his intention to fire. The monster froze, and then, to my grandfather's utter amazement, the broken and mangled face of a dozen different corpses spoke in a voice unbefitting its gruesome appearance and violent nature.

""Be calm, fearful man, or I shall be forced to extinguish the spark of life you carry within you!" The creature spoke strangely, and with an eerie calm, but my grandfather kept his wits about him, saying, "I know what you are. Leave this place or I will destroy *you*!" Grandfather backed up, pistol shaking in his hand, the weight of the beastly gun making his aim unsteady.

""I do not wish to harm you," spoke the monster before it was cut off by my grandfather. "Yet you have murdered many and likely will continue," he said. "How can one believe a murderer, particularly one with such clearly malevolent intents?"

"The Monster stood silent and pleaded with his hands, looking at his misshapen and malformed appendages. "My task on earth is not yet complete," it said. "I will allow no one to stand in my way before I have brought an end to my creator. He shall feel my pain as I drag him across this world toward the coldest, barest of places on God's earth. There will I end his life, and in so doing so allow mine own to end as well." My grandfather stood in awe of this thing before him, amazed that such a creature could live and breathe.

""How can you defend yanking a man's head clean from his body, or killing a youth in cold blood?" my grandfather asked the fiend who, in reply, raised his hands to his face and shook his head.

""Miserable wretch am I! He, my creator, was not aware of the power he gave me and I forget that I am not like any mortal man. I have the strength of twenty men and I forget how fragile humanity is. I attempted to but silence the one man, yet my hands tore him apart like he was paper in my grasp. As for the boy and the other, I merely defended myself. I am used to revulsion from man, but self preservation is still mine to keep, and I defend myself against arms. As you can see, they were not entirely unsuccessful." The Monster revealed a gaping wound on his side, and another down his arm--the suggestion of a bullet wound and the work of the young man's blade.

""I should destroy you and end your miserable existence!" my grandfather bellowed, but he did not fire at the fiend, for his wrath remained in check. As daemonic as the beast was, my grandfather knew of his woeful creation and the tragic tale of its abandonment. Yet, he could not help but feel a cold terror and sweeping sense of nausea whenever he glanced upon that unholy visage. He claimed the sight haunted his dreams to his final days.

""I will depart this region," bargained the creature. "My conscience is stained with blood and remorse and surely whatever my soul may be, it is destined for the long line of the damned and tormented. But I shall have company in my torture. Farewell, man. I must go north." And with that, the Monster of man's creation retreated into the forest and was soon lost in darkness."

Finished, Nathaniel sat back in his chair, the fire illuminating a contemplative look upon his face. The others shook themselves out of the spell under which they had been laboring.

"Did he ever encounter the Monster again?" young Abraham asked, well aware of the story's origins.

"No," responded Nathaniel. "I have heard rumors of its existence beyond its final supposed destruction in the far north. Those may be stories for another day, another time. For now, I will end with relating what happened to my late grandfather a few days after his encounter with the Monster."

He cleared his throat, the liquor having gone untouched for quite some time. The other three sat in silence, waiting patiently for the conclusion of the story. After a proper moment of anticipation, the young narrator continued.

"As I said, my grandfather had decided against telling the town about his encounter. He knew it was nigh impossible that he could explain that the fiend he encountered was one constructed from the bodies of the dead and given life by some insane European. Tales of phantoms and ghosts were par for course for this area, but a creature such as he encountered was far too real, and science was something few understood at that time. He kept his silence and worked his land, digging out the final crops, fearful of a brutal winter to come. He worked all day until the sun was low on the horizon and the night air chilled the ground and made his breath come out like fog. A man approached from the distance, a traveler--though likely not of any unnatural disposition. The man appeared tired and worn, the horse following behind carried a pack of supplies and what appeared to be several guns and other weapons. He could have been another hunter, or perhaps a member one of the former search parties now returning home from a great distance. But there was something off about his character, and he did not appear to be "from around here.""

"The man approached my grandfather and gave him a weak salutation. He spoke in a tired, accented voice, though his English was excellent and quite clear. He asked my grandfather where he was. My grandfather explained they were nearer Sleepy Hollow, and closer to Connecticut and further still, the Canadian border. My grandfather asked where he was from and to where did he travel at such an hour?

""I travel north, ever north, yet I know not where my final destination lies," said the man. He declined to introduce himself, but in truth there was no need for an introduction.

"The young man asked if my grandfather had recently encountered someone... extraordinary. My grandfather acknowledged that he had. No mention was made of the carnage this extraordinary man had left in his wake. none was needed. It was evident that the journey of creator and creation was one paved in blood.

""Forgive me, sir, all the trouble he has caused," pleaded the young traveller. "I will right this wrong even if I am to be damned for it. As surely I will." The man placed himself on his horse and bid my grandfather a good night before riding off toward the north and his destiny."

The audience sat in mesmerized silence.

"We have been haunted by phantoms and specters, witches and vampires," he said in summation. "Our region is one ripe for superstition and magic, but perhaps more horrible is the creation not of imagination but of man's own ambition. The Monster never had a name. He was abandoned before he ever was so christened."

Nathaniel rose to his feet. "His is a name that shall never die."

With a final swallow of brandy, Nathaniel crossed to the door, opened it wide, and vanished into the dark, merciless night.

MAYFLIES

By Ezra Heilman

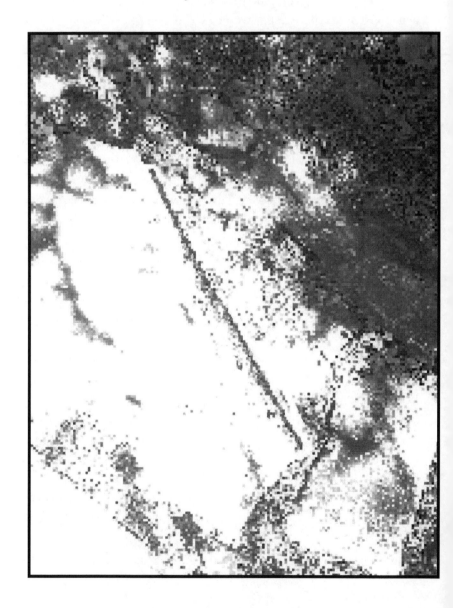

They just lay there, wings frozen on the cold, hard table like so much chaff after the winnowing. "They only live for a day."

"What's that, Gideon?"

"Mayflies. The schoolmaster told us so today. We were studying natural history," he said as he stared down at the two corpses. "It's so cruel. It seems so unfair."

"Life is God's gift, and He gives and He takes away as He sees fit," Mrs. Schuyler said between labored breaths. He could hear the rubbing of cloth against the washboard behind him. "It's not for us to know why the Lord does what He does, just so long as we follow His Commandments." Mrs. Schuyler paused to wipe the sweat from her forehead with her arm. "Gideon, come over here and light the lamp. It's getting dark."

"Is that why father died? Because the Lord took away?" he asked as he knelt at the fireplace.

"Your father brought it on himself. You see to it that you don't follow in his footsteps. Mind that you keep your feet on a righteous path. Otherwise, you're like to find yourself in a similar predicament."

She'd always admonished his father when he was alive for his lack of piety. George Schuyler had never bothered much to attend church on Sundays. It had been a point of disagreement throughout Gideon's early childhood. George provided well for his family, nevertheless, so his mother tolerated his lack of religiosity. When he started coughing up blood though, she'd said it was punishment from God for his years of iniquity. Gideon clenched his jaw each time he heard her say it.

Gideon reached into his pocket and took out a small wooden flute that had been all but concealed. It rolled in his hands. He let his fingers fill up the tone holes.

He heard Mrs. Schuyler drop the shirt into the bucket. She walked up behind him and bent over to see what he was holding.

"Where did you get that?"

"I found it in a tree."

"Have you been playing around in those woods again? I thought I told you to stay out of the woods, young man. Many a child has disappeared running off into the forests and hills. The Injuns used to practice heathen rites out there. You stay out of those wild places, or some pagan devil is like to catch hold of your soul," she said, waving her finger. "How many times have I told you, 'Idleness is the Devil's playground'?"

"I don't believe in the Devil."

"You'll believe well enough someday. The good Cotton Mather always said that only those who are ensorcelled by him deny the Devil's existence. You just watch yourself, mister."

"If there is a Devil, why would he be in our woods, anyway? And what difference does it make if I go there, so long as I do my chores, finish my homework, and say my prayers?"

"I'll be the one who decides what difference it does or does not make, young man." Before he could respond, she grabbed his chin and yanked his head towards her. "Why are you so pale? Are you getting sick?" She turned his head back and forth to examine him.

"I feel fine."

"You don't look fine. And you haven't had a healthy appetite for several days. Go wash up and get ready to say your prayers. You have school in the morn, and you need a good night's rest." He plodded off without another word. Feigning prayer was better than listening to her rebukes.

When the schoolmaster dismissed the children, he was first out the door. He was always the first. It was early November, and the skies were light grey. A horse-drawn carriage rolled past the schoolhouse just as he burst through the door. He trampled over the grass, running as fast as he could. Dead leaves stuck to the bottoms of his soles. The night's snow melt had left everything wet.

He reached the bridge in ten minutes. He turned south at the small stump, past the copse of great locust trees, over the great fallen elm, behind the abandoned mill, like a needle threading through the knots of denuded black forest--a mouse through a maze of grasping empty arms. Here, the lichen grew high on the trunk; there, the natural line of the trees curved to the east. After thirty minutes or so, the ground began to incline. He was getting close. The prickly wall of bush and bramble, all stripped of their foliage and flora by the autumn frost, came into view just over the last hill. He knew his way through this barrier as well. He'd traversed it many times. He reached for a high branch in the growth and found his footing. A few minutes later, he crested the brambles. He'd reached the top.

The hillock consisted of a small clearing in the woods. The remnants of a single great black oak, blackened by fire, stood off of the center. Gideon trampled the brown leaves beneath his feet. Everything was wet and dirty, except for the clearing. The knoll was empty when he arrived. It always was. This was where he'd found the flute, wedged into one of the curves between a dead branch and the stump of the large blackened elm. It looked as though someone had left it there for him. He took the wooden instrument out of his coat pocket and raised it to his lips. He ran his fingers over the "J" burned into the side. He raised it to his lips and blew.

The tones came slowly at first; then they coalesced into something corporeal. The wind howled in response. The dead leaves whipped into a frenzy around him and the trees sang.

A small bare foot stepped from behind the charred, black oak. "You're getting better," she said.

When Gideon returned home that evening, the sun was dying a deep orange fading into purple sky and then further to a deep blue. It blanketed the hills and forests of Sleepy Hollow from beyond the Hudson River. He heard the rhythmic creaking on the porch long before he could see what she was doing. His mother was knitting in her rocking chair. He walked past her and grabbed the handle on the door.

"Where have you been?" He turned and stared at her.

"Nowhere. I just went to the wooden bridge."

"The bridge? What were you doing there?"

"I go there to play my flute. I like the sound."

"Seems to me you've been doing a bit too much of playing that thing of late. You should be putting that energy into your hymns. If you're going to make music, it should be to the Lord," she said with a huff. "Well,

I was looking for you all afternoon. I was hoping you could take the candles I finished over to Reverend Jansen's house."

"Do I *have* to?"

"And why not?"

"Can't we just take them with us Sunday?"

"Now listen here, young man, you got this willfulness from your father. You see what it did to him. It put him in his grave, it did. And it'll do the same to you." Her voice shook as she spoke. "I'll not lose both a husband and a son to the Devil," she said, shaking her head so that her jowls shook.

"Father died of the cough. He just got sick. That's all,"

"You see! There you go--blaspheming. You're just like him. And what d'you think made him sick? It was his disobedience to God that made him sick. And the same's going to happen to you, if you aren't careful."

"Well, you can go without supper tonight. I'll see you in your grave before I'll let you live in disobedience to God under this roof." She rose and plodded off inside the house. He wasn't hungry anyway.

That Sunday the attendance at the Dutch steeple church was meagre. Why did his mother insist on dragging him here every Sunday while others stayed home? Gideon always objected. The bells rung as they approached the door. The Reverend Jansen stood at the door waiting for the last of his flock to scamper in. Usually, he and his mother arrived early, but he'd given her more trouble than usual that morning.

There was no lack of empty seats inside of the church this particular Sunday. His mother directed him towards a pew in the back. From the front, Mrs. Jansen looked back and smiled at his mother. Gideon's mother beamed back at her. Several minutes passed before the upturned corners of her lips relaxed. Gideon slid into the pew, and began to swing his feet beneath him. His mother glared at him.

Gideon turned his attention to the woman in the pew in front of them. Sarah Mandeville sat alone, as usual. He looked at the bruises on her arms. His mother said she was just clumsy. Mrs. Schuyler jammed a hymnal into Gideon's hands. From the left side of the church, Eleanor Gardner turned and smiled at them as well. Gideon's mother pretended not to notice. His mother never spoke to Eleanor. There were rumors about Miss Gardner that circulated amongst the women of Sleepy Hollow.

The Reverend Thaddeus Jansen walked across the platform towards the pulpit. He placed his hands on either side of the podium and cleared his throat. The congregation, comprised mostly of women from the town, stared up at him with rapt anticipation.

"Please turn to the book of James, chapter four," his baritone voice bounced off the walls as far as the back of the church.

"Today, I'd like to talk about that most precious gift bestowed upon man by the creator. I am, of course, talking about the gift of life. In verses thirteen and fourteen, the author of James says the following:

Whereas ye know not what shall be on the morrow. For what is your life? It is even a vapour, that appeareth for a little time, and then vanisheth away.

A vapour, and nothing more. The Lord has bestowed upon each of us a single spark of his divine gift. But it is our responsibility to be worthy wardens. We must not waste or squander what the Almighty has deigned to give. It is not ours to give, nor to take. It is our joy and our burden. Yet, we must remain ever mindful that the Lord God can take it back whenever he chooses."

When the reverend had finished his sermon, he asked the sparse congregation to bow their heads in prayer. This was Gideon's favorite part of the service. While the congregation bowed their heads in prayer, Gideon peaked around the church. He looked at the bruises on the arms of Sarah Mandeville. She, like so many of the other wives, attended alone most Sundays. He looked at Reverend Jansen. He looked at how the reverend looked down at Eleanor Gardner as the congregation bowed their heads in silent prayer. And he looked at his own mother, eyes shut tightly, as though she were afraid one might question the fervor of her faith.

As people shuffled out of the pews, Reverend Jansen waited by the door to say farewell. Mrs. Schuyler dragged her son into the aisle.

"My, haven't you *grown* little Gideon Schuyler," a playful voice asked from behind.

"Yes, Ma'am," he replied.

"Don't you feed your young man, Agnes? He looks so pale." Eleanor returned her attention to Gideon. "I hope you're not getting sick."

"I'm more concerned with his so--," Mrs. Schuyler began to reply.

"Hello, Agnes. Always so good to see you," Reverend Jansen interrupted. His mother recovered quickly.

Gideon turned to see the reverend take Miss Gardner's hand and cover it with his own as Mrs. Schuyler pulled Gideon behind her.

His mother and Mrs. Jansen hated Eleanor. His mother never failed to make a disparaging comment if Eleanor passed in the street or came up in polite conversation. Maybe that was why he liked her. Anyone his mother hated must have some redeeming quality about her. Something about her felt more human--more like the mother he wished he'd had.

Gideon stirred his porridge with the spoon, but his mind was clearly elsewhere.

"Where's your appetite?"

"I guess I'm just not hungry."

"Eat anyway. Why should I be embarrassed at church, by Eleanor Gardner no less, because you don't want to eat your food." She shoved spoonfuls of food into her mouth between chastisements.

"Are you coming down with something? She's right; you do look pale." She walked over and felt his forehead with the back of her hand. "Well, you don't have a fever. Seems you've had something awfully pressing on your mind these past days. Come to think of it, you didn't eat much last night either. Is your stomach bothering you?"

"I'm fine." He forced a spoonful of porridge into his mouth. "I'm just not hungry; that's all."

"You should be grateful there's food to be had on the table. It has something to do with that flute, doesn't it? Don't think I don't see how you handle it morning, noon, and night," she said waving her finger at him from across the table.

"Yes, mother." He didn't want to draw more of her ire.

He stomped across the open field in front of the stone, Dutch church, past the dale, and onto the path that led over the wooden bridge.

Each day as he passed the bridge, he returned to another world, where only he and Jane existed. They had their own little universe, and he didn't need to share her with anyone else. He wound through the forest like a drop of pink in tattered grey moving between the patchwork cracks of withered tree limbs. He could see it up ahead. The wall of brambles and forest detritus encircled the small hill. The top of the hill was brighter--as if the clouds parted just a little bit and the light shone more sweetly on the knoll.

He leapt on the withered underbrush, snagging a stocking in the process. His mother would yell at him later for it; he was sure. As he cleared the top, he fell to his knees on the thick blue-green grass.

He reached into his jacket and pulled out the flute. He raised the sound hole to his lips and began to blow. The pitches came easier today. His lips were getting stronger. His fingers were more nimble. Usually he had to play the melody several times, but this time he only played it twice. He wasn't sure where he'd heard the tune before, but it was as familiar as his mother's corned beef. When he finished the melody, he pulled the flute away from his lips. It had begun to snow, and Jane was standing across the patch of grass on the hillock. She wore a white simple gown, a blue ribbon in her hair and black shoes. She always wore the same outfit. Her eyes were deep sapphires--almost indigo if the light caught them just right. "I was waiting for you." She stepped forward from the oak. "I love the sound. I miss it so very much."

"I love it too. I want to stay here and play all the time," he said pushing a bunch of sweat-soaked, dirty-blonde hair from his eyes. He hadn't realized when he began to play that he hadn't yet caught his breath from the climb. The sweat froze on his skin.

"I'd like that as well. I don't think your mother would though." She cast her eyes down on the ground.

"No, I don't think she would. Let's not talk about her though." His gaze joined hers on the grass. "Would you like my coat? Aren't you cold?"

"No, I'm fine." She looked up and smiled. "Can you play some more? Can you play this?" She hummed a delightful minor-key melody in triple meter. It reminded him of the palaces he read about in the fairy tales. He'd never heard it before, but his fingers quickly found the pitches. It were as if the little wooden instrument taught him where the notes were. The empty tone holes beckoned to his little fingers.

He played the tune three times fumbling with fewer notes each time. The fourth time, he had the notes under his fingers. The fifth, he could play it with feeling. The sixth, he noticed the sound echoing back from the naked trees, resounding through the skeleton forest. The seventh--there was no seventh. The snow had begun to fall more heavily, and she walked over and pulled the flute from his lips. She put her hands in his and began to pull him in time to the melody around the grass circle--twisting and spinning, singing the tune as she spun him around the knoll. He'd never danced before, so it took him several turns to memorize the motions. She laughed at him as he tripped. The melody had never stopped, even though he was no longer playing. The notes wafted from the trees and forests, gliding into the circle with the flurries. They lilted and whirled 'round and 'round for time that seemed to forget itself. He wanted it to last forever.

"You shouldn't antagonize her. She'll only make it harder on you," Jane said, leaning on the grass across from him.

"I wish it had been her that died, instead of Dad. He's lucky. He doesn't have to listen to her anymore."

"You shouldn't say such things. Even if they're true . . ."

"It's hard living alone with her . . . without Dad, I mean. He used to protect me."

"Well, I'm here now. And if you listen, I can help you deal with her." She was only a couple of years older than he, but she felt much older.

"I want to come here and stay with you forever, Jane." He could feel her indigo eyes freeze on him. Her *mouth* smiled, but something in her eyes was sad.

It was dark and the full moon floated overhead through the cracks in the cumulus clouds when he returned home. Had his mother gone out? Maybe she was looking for him. The front steps screamed beneath his feet as he stepped up to the porch. He looked up and gave an audible start. Her pale face was behind the window. She stared at him. He opened the door and stepped into a gloom that saturated his clothes and his hair. "I thought I told you not to go to those woods anymore?" He turned to face her, sitting in the dark at the dining room table.

"I didn't."

"I'll not have you lying to me!" Her brow furrowed with rage. "I went to the schoolhouse today, and asked the schoolmaster. He said he saw you run off into the woods after school. I'd like an explanation. Why did you disobey me?"

"I don't know. I just like to get away. That's all. I finish my homework; I go to church with you every Sunday; I say my prayers . . . Christ, why do you have to dominate every part of my life?"

"Don't use the Lord's name in vain in this house!," she screeched, rising from her chair. "Dominate! How dare you?" she asked as she caught her breath. "I can't take it anymore. You disobey my rules; flout God's laws and use His name in vain. And now you're getting sick. Look at you. You're pale as a sheet." She walked over and touched his forehead. "And you're freezing. Where have you been?" She stood in silent vigil for his concession. The pregnant pause never came to term. "OK, have it your way. Tomorrow you can start packing your things. I'm sending you away." The gloom condensed on his skin.

"What do you mean?"

"I'm sending you to New York to live with my brother for a while. I'll not have some godless child running wild in my own home. If you won't respect me or my rules, then you can go live with my brother Philip in New York." she crossed to the writing desk and picked up the a quill pen off the desk and a sheet of paper.

"No, I won't go."

"You'll do as I tell you. Who do you think you are, telling your own mother what you will and will not do? You'll do as you're told."

"I can't. I mean, I can't go. I need to stay here." He gestured with his hands, looking around the room for the right words. "I need Jane!"

As soon as the words left his lips, he knew he'd erred. "You need *who*?" She dropped the pen on the parchment.

"Jane." His voice was a burst balloon exhaling its last puffs of air. "She's my friend . . . in the forest. That's why I go." She walked over and stared him in the eyes. Her eyes did not blink.

"Am I to understand that you've been going to the forest to sin with some wild, forest girl?" His face stung as it met the palm of her hand. "It's indecent! You are *never* to go there or see this . . . Jane again," she stared into his eyes as she waved her finger in his face. "Do you hear me? I won't have it. I suppose that's where the flute came from as well." She extended her hand. "Give it here."

"No, I won't." She raised her hand preparing to strike him again.

"I said give it to me! I won't tolerate idolatry in this house!"

He raised his hand to his face as he stared at her through tear-soaked eyes. "That's fine, Mother," he said as he clenched his jaw. "You won't have to." He turned, opened the door, and ran. Agnes Schuyler tried to follow, but by the time she reached the threshold, he was halfway across the field.

"Gideon!" she called. "Come back here! Gideon!"

The night he left home, a steady snowfall came to the valley just east of the Hudson River near the Tappan Zee. Mrs. Schuyler had run to the reverend's house first. When she told the Reverend Jansen that Gideon had run off into the woods and that she suspected he was participating in illicit behavior with a wild girl he'd met in the woods, the reverend dragged her to Sheriff Corwyn's house. The Sheriff and a few men he'd deputized rode out on the major roads to see if Gideon had taken the roads out of town, but there was no sign of him. The next day, the sheriff raised a posse to go out in the woods. Gordon Mandeville lent the party his hunting dogs, but the snow obfuscated whatever trail Gideon had left. Mrs. Schuyler spent most of that day with Mrs. Jansen. The Reverend had joined the rest of the search party.

It was evening before the search ended. The men returned that evening with dour faces. Sheriff Corwyn told Mrs. Schuyler the boy was probably long gone, and that he and his men had done all they could. Mrs. Schuyler pleaded with him to continue looking the next day. The sheriff agreed to go out once more in the morning.

Mrs. Schuyler returned home that night and knelt in her house praying to God for her son to return. She could hear the wind howling outside the house. Snow flurries fell steadily past the window. She remembered how sickly he looked the night before. She remembered his ghostly mien under the light of the full moon as he'd returned home. The withdrawn dark eyes. She couldn't sleep, so she remained on her knees in prayer deep into the night.

Mrs. Schuyler was still on her knees staring up at the large cross on the wall when she heard the pounding on her front door. It was late. Could it be Gideon? Why else would anyone come so early in the morning. She rose slowly, rubbing her knees, and limped towards the door.

"It's me, Eleanor--Eleanor Gardner." Mrs. Schuyler cracked the door. She looked Miss Gardner over from head to foot.

"Yes--what is it?" she asked with evident consternation.

"I heard what happened to your son."

"Yes? I'm sure everyone's heard by now. Is there something you can do about it?"

"Well, it's just that . . . I should have come sooner, I guess." Mrs. Schuyler's eyes widened. "You told some folks that Gideon had met a girl in the woods. You told folks her name was--Jane . . ." Eleanor's eyes moistened.

"Yes? Why? Do you know something?" Mrs. Schuyler asked.

"I think I know where Gideon is."

Mrs. Schuyler dragged Miss Gardner to Sheriff Corwyn's house and banged on the door. By the time the sheriff had raised the men, the sun had crested the horizon. The snow had stopped. Sheriff Corwyn had never heard of the place Eleanor described, but Reverend Jansen said he knew the way. Mandeville brought the dogs anyway, just in case. Mrs. Schuyler and Eleanor followed the party from the rear. The sheriff protested, but the two women were resolute. Eleanor was certain Gideon would be there.

The snow started again when they all convened before the barrier of brambles and dead trees. Reverend Jansen led the way, losing his balance only once. A drop of crimson fell on the snow below. He reached up and pulled himself the rest of the way without mishap. Sheriff Corwyn followed. Several of the men had to help Mrs. Schuyler and Eleanor over the thickly entwined thorns. Reverend Jansen was the first to see. He was soon joined by Sheriff Corwyn. Gordon Mandeville came next. One by one they arrived and formed a circle.

They looked down at something lying on the ground. Mrs. Schuyler was the last to clear the brush. Between the men's legs she saw the small, white leg and a familiar shoe.

She forced herself between the Sheriff and Reverend Jansen. She'd forgotten how much he looked like his father when he smiled. His blue lips were curled gently at the corners. His eyes lay open and clear, like his father the day he'd proposed to her. Mrs. Schuyler thought her son's eyes were somehow more beautiful now, as he lay there frozen in the snow. She looked down and in his hand he held the small, wooden flute. Mrs. Schuyler felt Eleanor press against her arm. Eleanor bent down to turn the wooden pipe in the boys hand. Mrs. Schuyler heard her gasp.

"God help us, that's impossible," Eleanor said, raising a gloved hand to her mouth. "This was Jane's! It was my daughter's!" She looked at Reverend Jansen.

"How can that be?" the reverend asked, in an airy, uncertain voice. "It was buried with her . . ." No one else said anything.

They all stood there for a long time, looking down at the small petrified body. They stood staring at those upturned lips of innocent joy--at eyes of tender satisfaction. They stood in befuddled disbelief. They stood in silent awe. Finally, one by one, each in turn dispersed his or her own way into the snow. Agnes Schuyler was the first. Reverend Jansen was the last. The sheriff sent his men later to fetch the body.

Gideon Schuyler had moved on from this life--flown away.

They remained.

A Local Superstition

Adapted by B. B. Stucco

The magnificent Lyndhurst mansion of Jay Gould basked in the warm glow of the fading sun reflecting off the Hudson. Music and laughter filled every room as hundreds of Manhattan's elite crowded the summer home of the immensely despised yet deeply respected (and even more deeply feared) railroad magnate.

Among the guests that fateful evening was young Miss Margaret Salt, the heartbreakingly-attractive young daughter of Mr. Edwin Salt, Esquire. Mr. Salt had dragged his daughter up to the country in hopes that her unsurpassed beauty would help sway Gould into doing business with him. Sadly for Mr. Salt, the billionaire had hardly looked at Margaret upon introduction, and she had quickly managed to run off to find entertainment elsewhere while her father doggedly and pointlessly pursued the owner of the estate.

Never one to want for company, Margaret soon found herself in the center of some of Manhattan's most eligible bachelors, as well as the young women following them around like puppy dogs. She absently adjusted the many long ruffles of her skirts billowing about her while holding court.

Normally Margaret would have thrived as the center of attention. Tonight, however, she was remarkably irked by the fact that the most eligible of the bachelors present--one Adam Samuels--appeared more interested in one of the silly puppy dogs circling the edge of Margaret's charisma. Even worse, Miss Pamela Sorenson was a local with an obnoxious accent and a dreary, breathless tone to her voice.

"When our carriage passed the cemetery on the way here," she droned, "our horses nearly reared up. Our man had a devil of a time getting them back under control. I was almost frightened out of my wits!"

"Which I'm sure would not have been a great loss," jeered Margaret, turning and smiling at her harem as a signal that they, too, should laugh at Miss Sorenson.

While most of the young Manhattanites obeyed, Adam, infuriatingly, spoke up in defense of the country bumpkin. "It certainly is a frightfully spooky cemetery. There are stories which claim it to be haunted, just as Washington Irving implied seventy years ago in his Legend of Sleepy Hollow."

Margaret groaned. "Oh come now, Mr. Samuels. That was a work of fiction. You don't really believe in ghosts, do you?"

"Don't you?" asked Pamela incredulously.

"Of course not," sneered Margaret. "We are a bit more sophisticated down in The City."

"There are plenty of people in Manhattan who would disagree with you, Miss Salt," said Adam. "In fact, my manservant told me quite clearly on the trip here that Irving, himself, is buried in that cemetery. And that his ghost is often seen roaming the graveyard late at night."

"Oh, honestly!" Margaret waved her hand in dismissal. "A local superstition, nothing more."

"Oh no, Miss Salt, it's very real," said Pamela. "You'll never catch me in the cemetery after the sun is down." She gave a shiver, and Margaret couldn't help but notice Adam put his arm protectively around the silly thing's shoulder.

"Why not?" pressed Margaret. "Are you afraid?"

"I think that's enough, Miss Salt," said Adam. "It's not as if you'd dare trespass Irving's grave after dark."

Margaret crossed her arms defiantly. "And why not? I'm not the one scared of a seventy year old wive's tale."

"Prove it!" shouted Pamela, pointing a finger accusingly at Margaret. "I bet you can't enter the cemetery alone. Tonight. Visit Irving's grave in the dark, if you dare."

All eyes were now on Margaret, who couldn't for the life of her comprehend how this foolish country coquette had turned the tables on her. Her would-be suitor waited to see if the haughty Miss Salt would take up the challenge or wilt under pressure.

Margaret Salt never wilted.

"With pleasure," she said, lifting her chin into the air. "Adam, if you would escort me to Sleepy Hollow Cemetery, please."

She put out her hand, but Adam stepped away and tightened his arm around Pamela.

"If it's all the same, Miss Salt, I have no desire to set foot anywhere near that graveyard tonight."

Margaret did her best not to flinch at his words, not wanting to be seen as weak in front of the others.

"I understand, Mr. Samuels," she said, her voice dripping with sarcasm. "A supposedly haunted cemetery is no place for a boy."

She then turned to her crowd of admirers to find a suitable chaperone, but one-by-one the young men found reasons to decline the honor. It seemed the perceived threat of a vengeful spirit outweighed the opportunity to spend half an hour alone with the incredibly beautiful Margaret Salt.

"Very well," she said, drawing herself up and exuding an air of superiority despite the evening's turn. "Since none of you has the stomach, I shall journey there on my own. I'm sure the dead will be better company than the cowardly."

With that she tossed her hair and made to walk away from the gathering, but was stopped by the gleeful cry of Pamela Sorenson.

"Wait!" cried the local girl, giddy with her triumph. "How will we know you've really been there? For all we know, you could simply walk away from Lyndhurst and return tomorrow claiming to have visited Irving's grave. We need proof."

Margaret scowled, both at the audacity of this young harlot to doubt her word and at the fact that she had, as it so happened, been thinking about doing just that. In what she considered a moment of inspiration, however, Margaret reached out and grabbed Adam Samuels' walking stick--a solid black staff topped by a comically elaborate claw--from the young man's grasp.

"Since it would seem my good word will not suffice, I shall plant this absurd cane in front of Irving's tombstone," she announced, holding the cane aloft for all to see. "In the morning, you may travel to the scene of my triumph once the sunlight has fortified you with the necessary courage to cross the threshold of the cemetery. Then you will spy the token you so desperately crave and know I am a woman of my word."

With that, Margaret Salt twirled away, expertly causing the many layers of her skirts to flare out behind her in an impressive display, and marched towards her chosen fate.

Her driver refused to take her all the way to the cemetery, so Margaret was forced to walk nearly a mile in the moonlight. To amuse herself, she pawed at the air with Adam's claw-topped cane, imagining she was gouging out the eyes of that meddling Pamela Sorenson. Margaret still found it unfathomable that a proper Manhattan socialite such as Adam Samuels would choose such a simpleton over Margaret Salt.

Reaching Sleepy Hollow Cemetery, she pushed open the iron gates with an unladylike grunt and strutted through. Within was silence and darkness. Ancient tombstones stood quietly in the moonlight, like sentinels at attention. Margaret knew the author's grave was beyond the church, so she hiked up her skirts and marched proudly over the entombed dead.

As she passed the church, however, Margaret felt her first quiver of anxiety. Perhaps it was being surrounded by so many final resting places, but she began to imagine shadows behind every tree and gravestone, and to hear whispers and murmurs in the air. She clutched Samuels' cane, admittedly thankful to be carrying something with which she could defend herself if the need arose.

Up ahead, she spotted the hill under which the American literary icon was interred. Steeling her nerves, she climbed the moist incline toward her destination, determined to complete her task and leave this accursed place.

After what seemed a longer hike than it should have been, she found herself standing at the foot of Washington Irving's grave. A slight breeze whipped about her, and all the sounds of the night imposed themselves upon her delicate ears. She forced her eyes to remain open and focused on the grave, knowing that if she dared close her eyes but for a moment, phantoms of the dark would surround her and she would lose her nerve and cut and run.

"I'm not afraid of you," she declared to the long-dead writer. Then she raised the cane above her head to thrust it deep into the earth in triumph.

She froze.

An elaborate moan echoed from beneath her feet. The wind, already teasing her locks, burst into a sudden gale. A stench of rot offended her senses. She could feel something approaching her from beyond the gravestone; something cold, foul, and inhuman.

Fear overtook her. True fear, the likes of which she had never known before. With the last remnant of her wits, she managed to stab Adam's cane into the ground while turning to run from the horror coming for her. But she was too late.

The incarnation of evil held her unyielding in its grasp and refused to let go. She could almost smell the putrid scent of its rotting flesh, but she refused to turn and look. Instead she struggled, frantic, as a panic welled up within her. She couldn't move an inch as the apparition tugged ever more tightly, holding her back. The more she struggled, the stronger the thing's grasp.

A gurgled scream came from her lips as she fell to her hands and knees, trying to crawl away from the abomination. But the phantasm that held her at bay tugged at her throat, cutting off her air. Spots forming in front of her eyes, she gave a final, desperate lunge forward. The grip on her throat tightened and refused to give way. Something erupted within her head, and she slumped to the ground. Blackness her only friend.

As the revel at Lyndhurst broke up, Mr. Edwin Salt searched for his daughter. It had been a poor evening, and he wanted nothing more than to return to Manhattan and lick his wounds. But Margaret was nowhere to be found, and no one could say where she had gone. Finally, Adam Samuels and a local girl admitted to daring Margaret to approach Irving's tomb. But that had been quite some hours ago.

Mr. Salt quickly organized a search party, and they rode out to the cemetery. This time the driver was not given the opportunity to pull up short. They arrived at the gates and raced into the churchyard.

It was Pamela Sorenson who found her first. Margaret lay face down on the earth not far from the grave of Washington Irving. She was dead, and her eyes, wide with fear, would haunt the local girl for the rest of her life.

The end of Miss Salt's skirts were pinned solidly into the ground by the claw-topped cane of Adam Samuels, while the clasp remained tightly wrapped around her bruised and swollen throat--evidence of her final, desperate struggle for breath.

She had been, quite literally, terrified to death.

Dead Men Rise

By Andrew M. Seddon

The rusty metal of the old wrought-iron fence bit into my palms as I braced myself against the railings, afraid that my quivering legs would give way in--I glanced at the luminous dial of my watch--five minutes.

Beyond the railings, rows of tombstones shone milky white in the pale light of a nearly full moon, while just over the rise, the brooding bulk of Muhheakunnetuck Farm lay grim and forbidding.

Beside me, my cousin Russell shifted from one foot to the other.

"Do you want to move closer?" he whispered.

"Are you nuts?" I whispered back, not moving my gaze from the ranks of grassy mounds.

"Maybe you're right," he said, and edged a few feet further back.

How could so few minutes take so long to pass? I wished this to be over. Or did I? Another part of me wanted the moment never to arrive.

I took another glance at my watch.

Three minutes.

Inside the fence, close to one of the graves, stood another figure, his black clericals making him seem as if he were but another of the shadows that crisscrossed the lonely hillside.

I heard the rustle of pages as he opened a book--I assumed it was the *Missale Romanum*--and began to recite. Only the whisper of his elderly voice reached me, like the rattling of dead leaves.

My knuckles ached. I tried to relax my grasp, but my hands refused to obey my will. Perhaps the pain would help me keep my grip on sanity.

I could turn away. Leave this accursed place. Try to believe the words of the poet Swinburne that *"dead men rise up never."*

But I couldn't, and I wouldn't.

Fr. Connor was here because of me. I owed it to him to stay.

And I? I was here because of Russell.

No. I was here because I couldn't leave the past alone. Because I couldn't forget what I had seen before. Because *"life has death for neighbor… ."*

Another glance. One minute.

My pulse pounded in my ears, drowning out Fr. Connor's voice. For a moment, my vision grayed, and I forced myself to slow my panted breathing.

Dead men rise up never...

Dead men rise up never...

I repeated the words beneath my breath as if that would somehow make them real.

A sudden intake of breath from Russell startled me, and then I saw it, at first no more than a faint haze as of thin mist emerging from the lumpy mound of the grave, but then like a slurry of congealed moonlight, twisting and writhing as it elongated into a bizarre parody of a human form...

I forgot the pain in my hands.

Forgot Swinburne's words.

Forgot everything.

Because, just as it had in my dream, the awful thing turned to face me...

It was all because I received, out of the blue, an invitation from my cousin Russell to be his guest at the rambling old farmhouse in the hills outside Sleepy Hollow that he had recently inherited from my Uncle Zachary. Owing to a handful of visits during childhood, I remembered it with trepidation--a maze of oddly-shaped rooms and long corridors, of gloomy corners and twisting staircases, where a sudden creaking in the shadows paralyzed the lungs and the limbs with dread in case something more than settling framework was lurking there... .

I had feared those family visits to the ancestral home and the unsettling feelings I encountered there; even my youthful spirit knew that something wasn't right about Muhheakunnetuck Farm.

Although I was fond of Russell, I don't recall being particularly distressed when a falling out between my father and his brother had resulted in Dad's uprooting our family from nearby White Plains to Asheville, North Carolina. Our two branches thus diverged, and so Cousin Russell's letter caught me by surprise.

Contact with him over the years had been sporadic and typically limited to a card at Christmas and--if it entered either of our minds--one at birthdays. I knew that Russell had gone into law, specializing in divorce, and had made enough money to retire promptly upon receiving his inheritance. In this I envied him.

He had never married, perhaps having been dissuaded by seeing the results of too many ill-advised unions. In this I had, unintentionally, emulated him.

My career path had landed me in northern Virginia, but at the time his letter reached me, having been forwarded on by my house-sitter, I was working on a project involving the expansion of a hospital in Nassau County. A long weekend in Sleepy Hollow seemed the perfect antidote to the frustrations of dealing with obtuse administrators with grandiose ideas in complete variance to the necessities of reality--plush carpets in birthing rooms, I ask you!

Although Russell was a firm believer in the ancient art of hand-written letters--at least where family was concerned--in the interests of time I emailed him a reply, received a positive response, and the following weekend took the train to Sleepy Hollow.

Russell met me at the station, a tall, angular man with short black hair, dancing blue eyes, and somewhat sunken features--the classic Bayard family trait, which suited him but that had done me no good at all. He had a habit of repeating everything he said two or three times, which, for the sake of brevity, I shall not reproduce.

"Jenny!" he exclaimed, bounding across the platform. "What a pleasure!" He wrapped long arms around me and squeezed.

"It's good to see you again," I answered, extricating myself from the tight grip.

He picked up my overnight bag, slung it over his shoulder, and pointed. "Car's over this way."

"Is Sleepy Hollow really haunted?" I asked as we climbed into Russell's black BMW convertible--a cool 100K, I guessed--and headed through town. "I mean, other than by the Headless Horseman? Because I've had more than my fill of headless bureaucrats lately."

Russell laughed. "The poor guy's become a victim of commercialization. I wonder if he knows!"

I returned his laugh. "But seriously?"

"Well," he said, "there's the bronze lady in the cemetery. She's supposed to cry, or haunt you if you kick her in the shins."

"I'd cry if you kicked me in the shins, too."

"But if you mean ghosts... there are more of them than you can shake a stick at."

"Seriously?"

"Seriously. Dozens of them between here and Tarrytown." He gave me a sideways glance. "I even have my own."

I started. "You do? Does he pay rent?"

He ignored my quip, deftly swerving around a texting teenager who had stepped into the road. "The third Sunday of the month, that's when he appears."

"He who?"

His lips thinned. "Not at the moment. I'll tell you tomorrow night. For now, just enjoy the drive."

"Waiting drives me crazy," I said, but he paid no heed to my complaint.

I was annoyed, but I felt some of my tension ebbing as the powerful car purred through the gently rolling countryside. I've always loved farm country, tree-lined roads, and deciduous forests. And May is a beautiful month.

Russell asked me about my work as an architect, my parents, my--non-existent--love life, and sundry relatives.

"I never really knew Uncle Zachary," I said.

"A bit of an odd duck, really," Russell said, "although I shouldn't speak ill of my own father. He wasn't a bad sort, all things considered, but I was glad to escape the paternal residence."

"But now you're back in it."

"But now it's mine." He turned the BMW into a curving drive. "And here it is."

The farmhouse was rambling, but that adjective hardly does it justice. The stone-built main building dated from the late 1700s, but subsequent generations had made motley modifications--another room here, a loft there, a passageway, a staircase--until it was a positive jumble of confusing twists and turns. It was, in short, an architectural nightmare.

But it was a nightmare that had been freshly painted, its chimneys and steps repaired, and its windows cleaned and gleaming. The lawn was trimmed, and new mulch surrounded flower beds.

"The old place looks better, doesn't it?" Russell said as I paused outside the heavy front door after he unlocked it.

That wasn't why I hesitated, but sensing that he desired approval, I said, "You've done wonders with it."

I took a deep breath as I stepped over the threshold.

Some old houses have an inviting air about them, but Muhheakunnetuck Farm--so called after the Iroquois name for the nearby Hudson River--wasn't one of them. It had a brooding air of senescence, as if a house--and I know this sounds strange--could have Alzheimer's disease. But it wasn't a benign senescence; rather there was an ill-defined sense of malignancy, yet a malignancy that had faded into a shadow of its former self, like an evil that was no longer active but only dimly remembered.

I had sensed it in childhood without knowing what it was, but now I could put a name to it. It made my skin crawl.

Russell conducted me through newly redecorated rooms filled with antique furniture--he pointed out a beautiful inlaid Renaissance buffet and a gorgeous Burgundian grandfather clock with obvious pride--to a bedroom on the second story. "I only use part of the house," he said as we mounted the stairs, "but feel free to look around as much as you wish."

I had no desire to wander through that house. Something of what I perceived must have shown on my face.

"You feel something, don't you?" Russell asked.

I nodded. "Don't you?"

He shrugged. "I grew up in this house."

I shook my head. How he could *not* detect the weight that settled like the oppressive heaviness before a thunderstorm?

He settled himself on the four-poster bed in what was actually an attractive room furnished with a dresser, a chest, and an armchair. The wallpaper was new, as was the carpeting.

"Why did you want me to come?" I asked.

He glanced up, his expression serious. "Back when we were kids you always seemed so level headed, so…"

"Boringly normal?"

His quick grin returned. "We come from a strange family, you and I. But the strangeness seems to have skipped you."

"Does this have anything to do with your ghost?" I wondered, not sure whether his last remark was intended as a compliment or not.

His gaze sharpened. "You were always quick-witted, Jen. Yes, it does."

"Then shouldn't you tell me-"

"First, I want to find out if you see what I do… or what I think I do."

"As long as you remember that I'm an architect, not a psychiatrist. I don't deal in visions or hallucinations."

He ran a hand along his brow. "I hope it's not a hallucination. I'd rather it were a ghost."

"How come I never heard about this supposed apparition before?"

Russell pursed his lips. "I don't believe our fathers ever spoke about it. Maybe it's just a goofy family legend. But I never saw it as a child… and that's why…" He broke off.

My chest constricted. "Look, Russell, I don't know that I'm the right person –"

He rose to his feet, interrupting me. "It's a lovely day. How about a walk? Work up an appetite for a Yankee pot roast."

"Suits me," I said.

Outside the house, the sense of gloom subsided and vanished completely as we strolled through an apple orchard listening to the hum of bees and the buzzing of insects. I needed to get out more, I told myself, inhaling deeply of the fresh air.

Muhheakunnetuck Farm was only a remnant of its former self, various parcels having been sold off over the centuries when a need for money arose. But a sizable amount remained.

I asked Russell what he intended to do with it.

"Keep it as it is, I expect," he replied. "There's no need to sell it or develop it."

I was glad to hear him say that, as so much lovely countryside was succumbing to development--perhaps a strange thing for someone in my profession to admit.

On a low ridge, a wrought iron fence enclosed a square of land.

"The family cemetery," I said, walking over. "I'd forgotten it existed."

I paused, studying the rows of tombstones. Some were still vertical while others leaned at drunken angles; a few still presented shiny marble faces, while most were encrusted by lichen and showed the weathering of years. And as I did so, a strange sensation, akin to what I had felt in the house, touched me like a cold, wet tendril creeping under my shirt and slithering up my lower back. I shivered.

"It's here, isn't it?" I asked softly.

Russell tried and failed to keep a flicker of surprise from crossing his face.

"Tomorrow night," he reiterated, the words sounding ominous, and led the way to a path that meandered through the woods.

The pot roast, served on Royal Doulton china, was delicious, and after dinner we relaxed in rocking chairs on the front porch, enjoying the cool evening breeze. Russell read a novel while I tried to focus on a crossword puzzle.

Later, he produced mugs of hot apple cider before I retired to wallow in a huge claw-footed bathtub and work out the knots that had mysteriously formed in my upper back.

I was afraid that I wouldn't sleep well in the house, despite the feathery-soft bed, and I didn't. It wasn't just the trepidation as to what I might--or might not--see the next day. Neither was it those childhood impressions resurrecting themselves from my subconscious and forcing themselves upon my adult mind.

It was as if the house didn't want me to sleep--as if it had aroused from its own troubled slumber and was regarding me with the decayed eyes of generations past, attempting to impress itself upon me... to seduce me, entice me, if necessary to compel me...

To what?

I didn't know.

I'd never had much interest in my family history. I had no idea what had transpired in this house to create the aura of brooding malevolence.

Unable to stand the sense of scrutiny, I jumped out of bed, parted the curtains and flung open the window. The soft touch of the nighttime breeze stroked my skin like the caress of a lover, while the moon flooded the hills with a gentle light. From this angle the cemetery wasn't visible, and for a moment, my fears abated.

But as I turned to return to bed, I wondered if I had made a mistake in accepting Russell's invitation.

"Did you sleep well?" Russell asked the next morning while laying out a hearty breakfast of bacon, eggs, sausage and hash browns.

"The bed was lovely," I replied, not wishing to admit to my nocturnal misgivings.

"Good." He sounded relieved. "I thought today I'd show you the sights: The Old Dutch Church, the Philipsburg Manor, the cemetery... ."

"Love to," I said, "but take me into Sleepy Hollow for Mass first."

"I forgot that you had gone Papist," he teased. "Not, of course, that you were the first."

"Only the first in our generation," I said.

Accordingly, he dropped me off outside St. Teresa's Church.

"I'm going to the country club to practice my putting," he said. "Be back in an hour."

Russell had always been punctual, and when I emerged from church an hour later, he was sitting on the hood of his car waiting for me.

We spent a pleasant day exploring the town, broken up by lunch at a tavern overlooking the Hudson River, and then dinner at a riverside eatery under the Tappan Zee Bridge.

"When do we need to be ready to see the ghost?" I asked as the sun disappeared and the rainbow of colors on the water of the river faded to gray.

"10:05," Russell said. "On the dot."

"I thought ghosts were unpredictable things--showing up whenever they wanted to, not bound by a clock."

Russell shrugged. "This one is punctuality... I was going to say 'embodied' but maybe 'disembodied' would be better."

I chuckled, more to hide my nervousness than from humor. "It will be a new experience for me."

We returned to the melancholy farmhouse, where, to pass the time, Russell regaled me with tales of Sleepy Hollow's other ghosts.

Eventually, he led me out onto the back porch from where we had an unobstructed view towards the ridge.

The moon, a few days shy of full, rose above the hills into a cloudless sky, casting pallid light across the fields and woods and illuminating the cemetery. The wind ghosted through the trees like something alive.

Russell checked his Rolex. "Almost time."

A thrill--or was it a chill?--tingled my nerves. I had never seen a ghost before, and I wasn't sure that I wanted to. Reading about them, or talking about them, was one thing; seeing one in the flesh--or *lack* of flesh, rather--quite another.

Maybe I wouldn't. Maybe Russell had been imagining things. He didn't *seem* crazy, but really, I hardly knew the man...

"Time," Russell said, and I tensed, peering at the cemetery.

At first, I saw nothing. Then...

Out in the family cemetery, something white, insubstantial, rose from the ground...

"Mist," I said, hating the shakiness of my voice.

"Watch," he said.

The mist elongated and assumed--it couldn't!--human form. My mind was conjuring shapes out of nothing.

I gripped Russell's arm hard enough that he gasped.

The figure writhed and twisted, straining upwards, stretching and extending as if reaching for the oblivious moon, becoming increasingly distorted like a character in one of El Greco's bizarre paintings.

And yet it failed to break free, tethered to the ground by an invisible cord.

At this distance I couldn't see its face--if it even had one--and yet I had the impression of a grotesque visage, distorted by pain and frustration, yet unmistakably Bayard.

And as I stared in horror, the tormented form retracted, losing its human likeness, as if being sucked back into the waiting earth.

Then it was gone.

My breath exhaled with a rush and I stood in silence for a moment, my legs quivery, my head swimming. A sudden cramp in my left hand reminded me that I was still clutching Russell's arm. Embarrassed, I let go, and reached for the porch rail instead.

"Flashlight," I said, forcing the word out.

"What?" Russell exclaimed.

"Flashlight," I repeated impatiently. "Have you got a flashlight?"

He slipped inside and returned with the requested object. I flicked it on and by its light made my way across the yard towards the cemetery, conscious of the hammering of my heart and glad for Russell following a few feet behind.

I paused for a second outside the wrought iron fence. What was I doing? This was the sort of thing that dumb people did in scary movies, and paid the price for.

Except that this wasn't a low-budget horror flick. This was real.

I became conscious that Russell was watching me. I had to be the sensible, level-headed Jenny that he expected me to be. Plus, I didn't like mysteries. I didn't like the unexplained. I preferred my world to be all neat and tidy, like a finished architectural drawing.

I thrust my weight against the rusty gate. It yielded with an ear-piercing screech and I crept in among the last resting place of the departed.

Which grave had the apparition appeared from? How could I tell? The perspective seemed so different by the light of the moon than in daylight. I circled the tombstones, jumping when a clump of tall grass tickled my ankles.

It was as I stepped close to one grass-covered grave, no different in appearance from any of the others that I felt it--the same sensation of withered malignancy that I'd felt in the house. And yet there was something else with it... something that I couldn't immediately identify.

"This one, isn't it?" I said, my voice sounding raspy.

"Yes," Russell said staring at me in amazement. "I had to watch from several different vantage points in order to figure it out."

I circled the grave, shining the light from one end to the other. "There's no opening," I said, more to myself than to Russell. "Nowhere for any kind of emanation or emission to come from." Russell might have preferred a ghost to a hallucination, but I'd sooner have discovered a more prosaic explanation.

I focused the beam on the weathered tombstone.

Malachi Bayard. 1785-1854.

The remainder of the inscription was indecipherable.

We retraced our steps to the house, and took seats in the living room.

"Drink?" Russell asked, pouring himself a shot of whisky and holding up a second glass.

"No thanks. Gives me a headache," I replied. "Tell me the story. Who was Malachi Bayard?"

Russell downed the whisky in a single gulp and stretched out his legs. "He was a brother of our great-great-great-great-great grandfather. I think I have that right. He lived in this house for some years before building his own place over the hill. It burned down in the early 1900s. He was not, it seems, one of the choicest apples on our somewhat misshapen family tree."

"Rotten to the core?"

"Perhaps not as bad as that," Russell said. "He was the family miser, and amassed quite a fortune in various business dealings--some legitimate and others apparently quite shady."

"Rich and unscrupulous?"

"And unpopular. He never married and had few friends. The only one who could tolerate him was his elder brother."

I leaned back in my chair. "You're quite the expert on family history."

"I was fortunate to discover this." Russell leaned to his right, plucked a book off a side table, and handed it to me.

It was leather bound, with a cracked binding and extensive water staining. I opened it carefully to find yellowing pages covered in immaculate copperplate script.

"It belonged to our five-times removed grandfather," Russell said in answer to my unspoken question. "Cyrus Bayard, older brother to Malachi, and patriarch of the family. It's a diary--a commonplace book, actually. Unfortunately, as you can see, there are pages missing, and many others are damaged. The mice had a field-day with it."

"Wherever did you get it?" I asked.

"I found it when I was rummaging in one of the unused rooms, stuffed into an old trunk."

I handed it carefully back to him. "So what does he have to say about Malachi?"

"Not a lot, actually," Russell smiled ruefully. "Unless there was more on some of the missing pages. But what he *did* say is interesting."

"Don't keep me in suspense!" I urged.

"Well," Russell said, "Malachi's talents as a noted miser failed to keep the Grim Reaper at bay, and one Spring he contracted a chill, which developed into pneumonia. I should mention that he had developed the curious habit of wearing a metal box chained to his wrist. He would never divulge the contents. Cyrus believed it contained some kind of charm which Malachi was too afraid or embarrassed to reveal. Anyway, when it dawned on Malachi that he was on his deathbed, he asked Cyrus to call for a priest."

"A priest?" I echoed.

"Strange, huh? Malachi doesn't seem to have been much of a church-going man, while Cyrus attended the First Reformed Church – now known as the Old Dutch Church. Well, what could Cyrus do but indulge his dying brother? He sent a messenger to fetch the priest. Malachi was well-nigh incoherent at this point, long periods of delirium being interrupted by brief spells of lucidity.

"There are some gaps in the narrative, but it seems that Malachi worsened rapidly, and uttered only a few more words, and those hard to understand." Russell opened the book and turned to one of the yellowed pages. "These were "poor", "bury", and "box." Cyrus took them to mean that Malachi wanted to be buried in a simple grave with his box."

"A reasonable assumption," I said.

Russell nodded. "Well, the priest didn't come. He'd fallen from his horse and broken his leg and was in need of a physician, himself. He'd been given enough laudanum that he was in no state of mind to do anything even if it had been possible to transport him to Malachi's bedside."

He laid the book back on the table. "So there you have it. Malachi died just after 10 pm on the third Sunday of June and was buried in the family cemetery. A traveling preacher performed the honors for a nominal fee, since it seemed that no one in town wanted much to do with Malachi. And it wasn't long afterwards that the ghost began appearing, which it has done regularly."

I thought for a moment. "What about Malachi's fortune?"

Russell gave a short laugh. "Who knows? They searched his house from top to bottom and found a fair number of gold coins, but nothing that constituted a fortune."

Something was jiggling in the back of my mind, but I wasn't sure what.

I yawned, my energy fading. "It's been quite a day. I'd better get some rest."

"Pity you have to leave tomorrow," Russell said.

"Work calls, and I can't afford to retire just yet."

"See you in the morning, then," he said, and I headed upstairs to bed--not that I was expecting to sleep well in this house.

And I didn't.

If the last night had been bad, this one was worse. After lying restless for a while, I must have fallen asleep, because I found myself drifting across a moonlit plain dotted with graves and skeletal, leafless trees, among which other shadowy figures flitted, too transiently for me to obtain more than a glimpse.

I was drawn to one particular grave, but as I approached, saw that it lay open, the earth mounded beside it, and nearby, a tombstone ready to be erected.

I scanned the eerie landscape, but I was alone, the other shadowy figures having disappeared. I tried to move away, but my dream-body wouldn't respond.

And then a movement arrested my attention. Something was emerging from the dark maw of the grave, something almost, but not quite human--or that had once been human.

It turned a hideous travesty of a face upon me--a face that grew and grew, dwarfing whatever semblance of a body it had possessed, until all I could see was a bottomless pit of a mouth from which mocking laughter erupted.

I swung away, only to confront a second figure rising from another grave, and going through the same transformation as the first. I pivoted again, and again, but each time another ghastly shape appeared before me, until I was surrounded by a ring of phantom mouths and the dreadful laughter screamed through my brain until I could bear it no more and-

I sat bolt upright in bed, clutching the sheets to my chest, drenched in sweat, peering into the dark corners of the room to assure myself that nothing was there…

And thus I stayed, too frightened to attempt to go back to sleep.

"You look awful," Russell said in the morning. "As if you'd seen a ghost."

I returned his feeble effort at humor with a bleary glare. "A bad dream," I said stiffly.

After a quick breakfast he dropped me off at the station. "Come again, sometime, won't you?" he asked, his blue eyes wistful.

"Sure thing," I replied, mentally vowing that if I did return to Sleepy Hollow I'd stay in a motel.

He gave me a quick hug, and I stepped on board the train.

A final wave, and then Sleepy Hollow was disappearing in the distance.

I leaned back in my seat, still puzzling over what continued to jiggle in the back of my mind. It was only as the train approached New York City that I suddenly understood what I had felt at the side of Malachi's grave.

And I thought I should do just as I would have done if a problem arose at work--bring in an expert.

I groped in my pocket for my phone and called Russell's number.

"May I come back next month?" I asked when he answered. "And bring a friend?"

"Certainly," Russell replied. "But who -?"

"Wait and see," I said, yielding to the malicious urge to make *him* be patient for a change.

It was a month later on a Sunday afternoon that once again I took the train to Sleepy Hollow. Russell met me at the station. We embraced, then his eyebrows rose as they lit upon my companion--a small, elderly man with a freckled face, the remains of sandy hair turned gray, who walked with a pronounced stoop and, most noticeably, dressed in black clericals and Roman collar.

"Allow me to introduce Father Rider Connor," I said.

Russell shook hands. "I must say, when you said 'a friend' I wasn't expecting an exorcist."

Fr. Connor chuckled. "Hardly that! I am merely a simple priest who takes an interest in the unusual."

"Fr. Connor is retired now, but we've known each other for several years," I interjected. "I told him the whole story since I thought he might have some insight into your apparition."

"And do you?" Russell asked the priest.

"I believe so," Fr. Connor said.

"Well then," Russell said, "let me take you to the scene."

It wasn't long until we were pulling into the drive to Muhheakunnetuck Farm.

"A charming location," Fr. Connor commented appreciatively.

"It suits me," Russell replied. "I'm just not so sure about having a ghost on the premises. Even a family ghost."

"Over there, I presume?" Fr. Connor gestured towards the cemetery.

Russell nodded.

Fr. Connor took off at a slow shamble.

Russell gripped my arm and held me back. "Are you sure about this?" he whispered.

"Fr. Connor is very astute," I whispered back. "And didn't Malachi want a priest to come?"

"A little late now, I should think," Russell retorted.

"Better late than never," I said, and a puzzled expression crossed Russell's face.

Fr. Connor waved us back as we approached the cemetery. "Don't tell me," he said, as he opened the gate and moved among the tombstones.

"This one, I think," he said, finally halting besides Malachi's grave.

"Yes," Russell answered.

Fr. Connor stood still for a moment, then his eyes met mine. "I believe you're correct," he said.

Russell looked perturbed. "What is it that you two can sense that I can't?"

Instead of answering directly, Fr. Connor said, "We must dig him up."

"Now just a minute!" Russell exclaimed. "We can't do that!"

"Father!" I said, equally shocked.

"We can and we must," Fr. Connor said.

Russell had gone pale, and I expect I had also.

"Malachi is unquiet," Fr. Connor added.

"Yes, but he's dead!" I protested. "Can't you just sprinkle a little holy water or something to make him go away?"

"No. There's something holding him back."

"Are you suggesting," Russell waved his hands, searching for words, "that Malachi's spirit is somehow stuck here?"

The priest nodded.

"It's insane!" Russell expostulated. "Jen, tell him!"

I sucked in a breath. Was I going to trust my friend, or not? "Even if Malachi wasn't the most reputable member of our family," I said, addressing myself to Russell, "shouldn't we help him?"

"How do you help a ghost?"

"Fetch a shovel, cousin," I said. "Better yet, two."

At first, I thought he was going to refuse, then he turned away and headed towards the house, returning in a few minutes with a pair of shovels, one of which he handed to me.

My palms sweaty, I dug mine into the ground, while he hesitated. "Come on, Russell," I said. "Or are you going to let me do all the work?"

With singular lack of enthusiasm he complied. My heart was racing as I toiled. I felt like a Victorian grave robber. While we dug, Fr. Conner took out a few things I recognised--rosary beads, a cross. He spent a lot of time murmuring in what I assumed was Latin. I hoped that he knew what he was doing.

What would Malachi look like after a century and a half in the ground? Would the climate have preserved him somehow? Or would he be there, all rotten and moldy, decaying like a zombie? I choked back a surge of nausea.

Fortunately, recent rain had made the ground soft, and the digging was fairly easy. Still, my shoulders and arms were aching by the time we reached six feet under, and something that wasn't soil turned up.

Of the coffin, nothing remained but corroded hinges and some discoloration of the earth. And of Malachi himself--to my relief, only dis-articulated bones. I averted my gaze from the grinning skull. Looped around the forearm bones was a chain, and attached to that, a metal box. My hand trembling, I gingerly picked it up, ignoring the seemingly disturbing gesture the bones seemed to form as I shoved them aside, and handed it to Fr. Connor.

"Look," said Russell, "doesn't this amount to desecration?"

Fr. Connor shook his head. "Quite the opposite."

He knelt by the side of the hole and removed a vial of oil from his pocket.

"The dust returns to the earth as it was," Fr. Connor said, "and the spirit returns to God who gave it."

He anointed the skull and some of the other bones, reciting the last rites as he did do. When he had finished, he rose, dusted off his knees, and said, "Let's cover him back up."

"Gladly," Russell said, shoveling dirt back into the hole with far more alacrity than he'd removed it.

When it was covered, we traipsed back to the house, where Russell retrieved a hammer and chisel from his toolbox.

"Not just yet." Fr. Connor laid his hand on the box and slid it away from a surprised Russell. "First, I want you to give me full discretion to deal with the contents of the box as I see fit."

Russell's eyes widened. "That's asking a lot."

"It is," Fr. Connor said.

Russell looked to me for support.

"Father –" I began.

"I assure you, it's quite necessary," Fr. Connor said.

After a long moment, Russell shrugged. "What am I going to do with a decrepit old charm, anyway? Alright."

"Second," Fr. Connor said, "let's wait and see what happens tonight."

"In that case," Russell said, apparently having shaken off any adverse effects from the grave-digging, "who wants a drink?"

The time until ten o'clock seemed to crawl by, despite engaging conversation and an impromptu piano recital by Russell on his Steinway that made me wish that I had practiced more as a youngster and could afford my own.

But finally the sun slid behind the hills, and the sky darkened into a cloudless and crystal clear night.

"Pony up," Russell said at last, and led the way across the meadow, Fr. Connor and I following. Russell walked stiffly, probably as tense as I was. Fr. Connor carried a thick black book under one arm, and I noticed his lips moving silently as he limped up the rise.

The graveyard felt even more bleak and desolate at night than it had during the day, the slanting tombstones shining eerily, like a strange, silent congregation somehow waiting for us.

Fr. Connor walked through the gate. "Coming in?" he asked.

I'd mulled over what I would do. "No," I replied. I don't think anything could have convinced me to pass through that gate.

I clutched the railings and peered into the blackness as the minutes ticked slowly past.

And then it appeared-

-it turned to face me, and for an interminable instant of fear I stared into the distorted visage of what had once been a Bayard, its features warped by endless years of desolation and despair and frustration-

"Russell!" The voice was mine, though seeming to come from far away. "Do you see?"

-before it twisted and turned as it strained upwards, elongating, hands extending into the night sky as if trying to grasp something that was barely out of reach...

And I fancied I heard mocking laughter, as in my dream.

But then over it I heard Fr. Connor's voice, now firm and confident, and the scathing laughter faltered-

The writhing form stretched farther and farther--how long could this go on?--until it reached the point where it could stretch no more, and there it hung, suspended between earth and sky. Surely, as before, it must be sucked back into the ground.

"Ego absolvo vos…"

To my astonishment, the spectral form snapped.

Enveloped in what I can only describe as a golden shimmer, it surged upwards and was gone.

I collapsed against the railings, breathing heavily, conscious of nothing else until a hand touched my trembling shoulder, and I looked around to see Fr. Connor standing beside me.

"Are you alright?" he asked.

Too shaken to speak, I only nodded.

He held me by one elbow and Russell by the other as we made our way back to the house.

"Now," Fr. Connor said, sounding business-like, "let's open the box."

It felt like an anticlimax as we sat around the table while Russell, pale and subdued, set to work with his hammer and chisel. A few deft blows shattered the lock, and he pried the lid open.

I gasped as gems poured onto the table. Diamonds, emeralds, rubies... a king's ransom.

"The missing fortune!" Russell exclaimed, running his fingers through them. "Not a lucky charm after all! Talk about hitting the jackpot!"

"Russell–" I began, imagining myself not having to work anymore, not having to deal with bone-headed administrators whose fantasies outstripped their capital...

His glance at me lacked warmth. "Of course, you can have a share as well," he said, in a grudging tone. He neatly divided the pile in two and pushed the smaller half towards me.

Fr. Connor cleared his throat.

We both looked at the priest, who was shaking his head.

Russell's jaw dropped. "But..." he stammered, "but you can't. I mean, these are mine..."

"They would do you no good," Fr. Connor said. "You either, Jen."

The look in his eyes was dead serious. I knew he was right.

And yet...

"Why not?" Russell asked, his voice harsh.

"What I felt," Fr. Connor replied, "while standing at the grave, and what Jen also detected, was not only the essence of Malachi's bad deeds but also an impression of remorse."

"I don't see Malachi as the repenting type," Russell scoffed.

"Nevertheless, he performed the uncharacteristic action of sending for a priest on his deathbed," Fr. Connor pointed out, "which implies some change of heart. And remember Malachi's last recorded words," he added, his focus shifting between us. "'Poor', 'box', and 'bury'. Everyone assumed that they meant he desired to be buried with his box. But taken together, they suggested to me he wanted to be rid of the box--that he didn't intend it to be buried with him at all. Unfortunately he was unable to communicate his desires in an understandable manner. And so he was buried as we found him."

"It's crazy," Russell said.

"Not at all," Fr. Connor countered. "I am convinced that Malachi realized what his attachment to wealth had done to him, and desired the contents of his box to be given to the poor. And that is exactly what I shall do with them."

His gaze took in both of us. "There will not be another Malachi." He reached out to sweep the gems away.

"No," Russell said. His cheeks flushed as he blocked the priest's move. "This is a plot, isn't it? Jen, how could you? You knew what was in the box, and you're trying to rob me!"

For a moment, I wavered. What I could do with the money those gems would provide... .

And I felt Muhheakunnetuck Farm gloating, as if all those warped and twisted scions of the family tree were reaching out to embrace me into their perverse fold...

In my mind's eye I was back in the cemetery, observing the struggles of a blighted spirit, confronted by that haunted face with its tormented eyes and expression of sheer hopelessness... and I shuddered, realizing the awful fate that lurked for me in the darkness of my own soul.

And not only me.

"He's right, Russell," I said, forcing myself to speak. "Did you see, tonight, the face...?"

"No," he said, in a tone that made me doubt his veracity.

I reached out and with quivering fingers slid my portion of the gems over to Fr. Connor.

"I did," I said, uncomfortably aware that I possessed more than the Bayard physiognomy, "*and in it I saw my own!*"

THE SECRET OF
PENDELWOOD COURT

By Michael Nayak

Richard was flying out to Los Angeles for his next symphony concert, and Alice asked him if he wanted a ride to the airport. She could pick him up, too, if he wanted.

Alice genuinely enjoyed the tall, brooding man's company. There was so much more to him than met the eye. Every time she peeled back a layer, ten deeper layers waited to be discovered. But she was nothing if not practical. She was due back at the *New York Post* in September, and her time was running out. She needed to know the truth about what he was hiding, and her editor was not a patient man. So after driving to the airport, she drove back to his house, kicked her heels off, and climbed over the tall fence into his backyard.

And suddenly, so quickly it was like an icy fist had been thrust right through her, she went cold. Her skin sprang to life--a thousand invisible ants crawling beneath her chilly skin. Her pounding heart clamored with irrational fear. Here, behind the tall fence that cut off the neighborhood, it was a different world.

There was madness here.

She took a deep breath to try to center herself and approached the back porch. Her bare foot caught on the single, aged step and almost rolled. Regaining her balance, she looked down and a soft cry escaped her lips. The deep gouge marks in the wooden step were impossible to miss--they gave off the impression of an animal with sharp claws being dragged backward into the house. *Something huge.*

The feeling of dread intensified as she stepped closer to the door. There was something electric in the air, something that sizzled of fear. Her hand slowly reached out for the brass door handle. She could feel her breath in her ears and taste her dry mouth. Closer and closer, her fingers tensing –

A snap of electricity bit into her hand as she made contact with the handle, and Alice jumped back with a shriek. She tripped, arms cartwheeling frantically, and fell backward, crashing down so hard on the loose boards of the wooden porch they jumped up from the impact. The world grew darker, she moaned, and then everything was silent.

Alice was not without her wiles. She had been manipulating people for most of her life, and it was a role in which she felt comfortable. In a dog-eat-dog world, a girl with good looks and not much in the remorse department could go far. And in a time when people posted what they ate for breakfast on the Internet, a world-famous author who kept out of the spotlight was a front-page story waiting to happen.

"Not a hell of a lot," Stu had admitted when Alice had asked him about the reclusive author. "All I know about the guy is the return address on his envelopes. M. MARTIN, Pendelwood Court, Sleepy Hollow, New York. All his mail goes directly to Sandra Locke; no one else sees it."

"Pendelwood Court, did you say?" she murmured.

Alice had met Stu at one of the many lounge bars scattered around Manhattan, where white-collar professionals tried to coerce each other into bed against the soundtrack of subdued jazz and expensive drinks. She was an intern at the *Post*; Stu was an intern at the noted literary agency Locke & Shutte. He gave her his number; she said she would call and never did. A month later she got thrown an assignment: background on author Michael Martin, in anticipation of the release of the final movie in the phenomenally popular "Sleepy Hollow" trilogy, based on his books. It was supposed to be a quick Internet research project with her write-up due the next day.

But despite trolling for hours, she found no pictures of M. Martin anywhere online. Though a best-selling author with a three-movie deal, Martin had appeared at no book signings, premieres, or late-night talk shows. There were a few high-profile newspaper interviews, but when Alice followed up with the journalists she discovered the interviews had all occurred by e-mail. Even Martin's books didn't have a picture of the man, just a bare sketch of a biography: *Ever the nomad, between travels M. Martin calls Sleepy Hollow, New York, home.* The only contact information she could dig up for Martin was his agent: Sandra Locke, of the noted New York firm Locke & Shutte.

She turned in her write-up, and decided it was time to give Stu a call. She was not without her wiles, after all.

A week after her penultimate semester with the *Post* ended, she rented 79 Pendelwood Court in Sleepy Hollow, New York.

The wind took Alice's breath away as soon as she climbed out of her car, driving into her throat and drying it up. A light dusting of snow, so faint to be almost imperceptible, was coming down across her car, now sitting in the driveway of 79 Pendelwood Court. The U-Haul truck behind it split the dazzling rays of the sun into sparkles off its edges. By the time the evening sun had retreated behind it, she had met most of the other residents on the small cul-de-sac.

"Just moved here from the city," she told her visitors, with a wide, friendly smile. "Can't wait to get to know Sleepy Hollow!"

On the surface, Sleepy Hollow seemed your basic Hudson River village. On account of M. Martin's books--and the movies they'd spawned--it had more than the average village's share of tourists, but other than that, it was like any place else. There were pockets of wealth, mainly in 'The Manors' (Philipsburg Manor and Sleepy Hollow Manor), and pockets of the less fortunate closer to the downtown area. Pendelwood Court was located in Webber Park, a moderately-priced family neighborhood, priced just low enough to be tantalizingly (if impractically) affordable yet high enough to keep the 'riff-raff' out. Alice would never have been able to afford the rent without the help of Daddy's wallet, but she felt the possible reward for an exclusive interview with the reclusive author was worth diving into Daddy Debt. The denizens of Pendelwood Court were friendly but mildly distant. All in all, it was a near-perfect slice of suburbia. Yet somewhere on this quiet little street, one of the most famous authors in the country lived in deceptive mediocrity.

The leading suspect as to the secret identity of M. Martin quickly became Richard Tiwariya. He was the only one on the street who hadn't come over to introduce himself, so Alice marched across the street armed with a sweet smile and a prepared inquiry about the local area.

She knocked on the door, but there was no response. As she waited, she noticed all the curtains were drawn. Not just drawn, but pinned together. She backed up a step, and saw the windows on the upper floor were the same.

She knocked a second time. Still no response, but a car was in the driveway, implying the secretive man was indeed inside. She rang the doorbell insistently till he opened the door, a scowl on his face.

"Hi, there!" she said brightly. "My name's Alice. I just moved in across the street. Number 79. Just wanted to stop by and say hello!"

He smiled, but with a clenched look on his face. "I'm sorry. Now isn't a good time," he said.

"Oh, I understand," she chirped. "Tell you what, why don't I stop by later tomorrow?

She ignored his responding scowl and turned around and walked back down the driveway before he close the door in her face. When she finally heard the door shut softly but firmly, she risked a quick glance behind her and took note of the tall privacy fence erected around the back porch, cutting it off from the lawn. A hefty lock sat on the fence latch, denying access to the rear of the house.

A background Internet search that night on Richard Tiwariya dead-ended quickly. He'd graduated with a degree in music studies from Kansas State and went to work for Disney Animation Studios as a background music artist. He continued to excel in classical music and landed a gig with the New York Symphony Orchestra, with whom he had been a concert pianist for the last five years.

True to her word, she arrived at his door the next day. He seemed to be in a better mood, so after some very brief chit-chat, she fabricated an excuse to leave and invited him over that evening, again walking away before he had a chance to respond. Fingers crossed, she hoped her ploy would work.

She was pleasantly surprised when he arrived on her doorstep that evening, bearing a large pie that looked homemade. "I was just making dinner," she lied. "Come in and we'll have that for dessert."

He was polite yet reserved, talking down his achievements with a self-effacing latitude. When she asked him how old he was, he asked, "How old do you think I am?"

"Forty," she said. She already knew how old he was, but the lines around his eyes and whitening hair hinted at the other side of fifty.

Richard threw his head back and laughed deeply. "Thank you for being nice," he said. "It's okay, you can say it."

She shrugged. "Closer to forty-five?"

"I'm thirty-one," he replied.

"What!" she exclaimed. "No way!"

"Lifetime of worry, I guess. I don't mind. People say I look distinguished."

Alice worked the night, angling for an invitation to his place. Richard, however, proved deft at resisting her implied advances. "Sounds like you don't want anyone seeing the inner workings of Richard Tiwariya," she teased, though her playful tone was slightly diminished from frustration.

He laughed mechanically back at her. "Think of it as my temple," he said, an obvious attempt to change the subject. She noticed he didn't correct her.

It all fit so perfectly, she thought. M. Martin had never appeared in public, never given a TV interview, never been to a movie premiere. And here was Richard Tiwariya, who didn't want to invite his neighbor over to his house.

She continued to develop a friendship with him over the next few weeks. No one else fit the profile as well as he did. Artistic--he was a musician. Reclusive--even when she hinted she might be interested in him as more than just a friend, Richard didn't bite and invite her over. And finally, tortured. She could feel it coming off of him in waves. The man was miserable, yet didn't manifest his angst in any of the obvious ways. A man so miserable must have had an outlet for his emotional distress. Perhaps therapy.

Or perhaps writing a gripping trilogy of successful horror novels.

Like most of M. Martin's readers Alice had been moved to tears reading his books. Raised in an affluent neighborhood, she didn't have much in the way of childhood trauma. But reading his books, she felt transported. Sucked into the pages to the point she wasn't sure if she could tear herself away from them without leaving something behind. The words reached out to her and she felt the characters' pain as if it were her own--alien as she was to their situations and backgrounds. She laughed with them, cried with them, and upon reaching the end of one of his books, felt utterly spent. As if she had lived every page. The bitter ending of the final book in the trilogy had ripped her open with its pathos and heartache. Someone had lived that story, and it had not ended well. Yet it had been painted vividly, with an echoing familiarity that shocked her. More than anything, that emotional resonance made her want to know what made Richard Tiwariya/M. Martin tick. What was his demon?

But there were also practical reasons for getting closer to him, and she was nothing if not practical. No one as successful as M. Martin hid from fame unless he had a secret... and a famous author's secret could be an aspiring journalist's job offer.

Alice quickly understood she wouldn't lure Richard using the same bait that knocked men her age senseless. Mentally, he was as old as he looked. The scars of whatever he had been through marked everything he did. She settled for familiarity. Over the course of the summer, weekly dinners at her house became something of a ritual. Every Thursday, she would knock on his door to invite him to dinner on Saturday. The second time she showed up, he tried to buck the pattern she was setting, but she was ready for his withdrawal, and refused to take no for an answer.

"Your house always smells so good," he told her out of the blue one evening in late June. "I've developed this Pavlovian response to ringing your doorbell. My mouth is already watering."

"I think that's the nicest thing you've said to me yet," she laughed over her shoulder.

Unwillingly, almost painfully, Alice and Richard became friends over the course of their weekly dinners. She sensed his hesitation, even nervousness, at entering into a co-dependent relationship of some kind, however nebulous, yet she blatantly refused to concede to it. Every Thursday she knocked on his door, and every Saturday, he knocked on hers in return.

As he became familiar with being in her company, the relaxed Richard Tiwariya came out. The dark humor and self-effacing wisecracks hit her as a total surprise. He was quiet and reclusive, but not by nature, she realized. The artificial distance was a constraint he forced upon himself. As the weeks went by, his constant brooding began to soften in her presence, to the point where she found herself seeing him in a different light. He could be funny in a very dark way, and at times even charming.

The first week of July, he told her that concert season was starting up again. "So what does that mean for you?"

He shrugged, with a wry smile. "It means I travel to a different city for two days and a night every week, and play in a concert hall that looks exactly the same as the one the week before. But it also means I have to ask if you're free for dinner on Sundays, instead of Saturdays?"

Alice knew this was a major victory for her. He could have just canceled, but in some way Saturday nights had turned into the only true social interaction either of them had. This wasn't a surprise as far as Richard was concerned, but Alice was a little shocked when she realized it was just as true for her. Though Sleepy Hollow was no NYC when it came to nightlife, she had plenty of opportunities for a social life. That she had unconsciously limited herself to her interactions with Richard came as a surprise.

"I can work that out," she smiled. "On one condition."

He cocked an eyebrow. "Should I brace myself?"

"I'd like to see you play one of these days. Not any day in particular, just at some point it'd be cool to see what you do for a living."

He nodded, seriously. "I would love that. Music is maybe the one thing I legitimately think I can do. People, life, relationships--that's all hard. But music is beauty within reach. Don't get the wrong idea, though! I'm just one small piece in a large orchestra–"

"Don't worry, I don't snore too loudly."

She genuinely enjoyed Richard's company, but she was due back for her last semester at the *Post* in September, and her time to get her scoop and prove her worth was running out. So in early August, she drove Richard to Westchester County Airport, then sped home and jumped the fence into his backyard.

A snap of electricity bit into her hand as she made contact with the handle, and Alice jumped back with a shriek. She tripped, arms cartwheeling frantically, and fell backward, so hard the wooden porch crashed and jumped. The world grew darker, she moaned, and then everything was silent.

When she awoke, it was dusk.

The fence towered above her, unfriendly and foreboding. Alice groaned as she rolled over, feeling the back of her skull explode with dull pain. She dragged herself to a kneeling position, and realized that her fall had left a small stain of blood on the deck, darkened and mottled in the waning sunlight.

Then she heard the howl.

It came from inside the house, muffled yet high and crazed. Visions of maddening moons and devilish lakes and scratching her skin till it bled flashed through her mind till she put her hands on her ears and screamed for it to stop.

The howl died with an abrupt snap, and Alice felt physically sick. It took all her strength to clamber back over the fence, and she promptly threw up on the other side upon hitting the ground. A light breeze tugged at her hair, bringing her the sweet smells of the approaching Fall. She looked up at the twinkling stars and lazy clouds streaming across the sky--the perfect picture of beauty and contentment. Then she thought about the bloodstains on the porch and that terrible, muffled howl, and ran back home to three sleeping pills and a night full of tangled dreams that left her sweaty and disheveled.

She spent the remaining days before Richard's return agonizing over what she had experienced. She would peer at his house through her curtains time and again, as if expecting to see a monster glaring back at her from across the street. What was Richard hiding over there? Did she really want to find out?

She thought about all of this as she drove to the airport to pick him up, nervous to see him again. Had she really heard that howl, or had it been the result of her fall? A possible concussion, even? The pragmatic Alice took control. *You're being silly, girl,* it told her. *A simple case of static electricity knocked you down. You hit your head. That's all.*

Richard was in a good mood as they drove back across Westchester. The concert had gone very well, he told her. "It's always a pleasure to play in San Diego, especially when you get to the hall early enough to not be stressed about traffic."

"Yeah, that can suck," she replied, mechanically.

He looked at her. "Are you alright?" he asked. "You seem a million miles away."

"Do I?" She forced a smile onto her face. "Sorry, just preoccupied. In case you're wondering, this is what you are like all the time."

He laughed. "Well played."

"So listen, I didn't have time to cook tonight. I just got caught up with work stuff. So..."

"Perfect," he declared. "This gives me a chance to return the favor."

She looked at him, surprised. More than surprised, a little scared. Dinner at his house? She suddenly felt ill at the thought of returning there, hearing that howl-

"Let me buy you dinner," he said, oblivious to her instant sigh of relief. "'I know a great steakhouse."

It was almost like a date. He cracked jokes, returned her innuendo, even picked up the check. And yet, she couldn't enjoy herself. The more she dwelled on it, the more real the howl became. It reverberated in her memory, picking up steam, magnifying, taking on another dimension.

Became human, even.

The next week, after Richard flew off to his next concert, Alice returned to his house.

The dried patch of blood was still there on the back porch, a dark reminder of her last visit. She stared at it for a long moment, then crouched down on the porch, noticing a low-set window.

Hesitantly, she pressed her face up against it. It was barely above ground, and she lowered herself even more, placing her stomach on the wooden planks of the porch and trying to peer through glass against the glare of the sunlight behind her.

The glass was blacked out.

From the inside.

What the hell was down there?

A soft laugh rang in her ears and she leaped to her feet, head jerking around. There was no one. She was alone on the porch.

The doorknob again shocked her with static, but she was ready and ignored the slight sting. The door itself was locked, but she didn't let that stop her. Living in New York City and attending the school of unethical journalism had taught her a few tricks. She knew how to deal with a cheap snaplock.

The door creaked open, and she stepped inside.

The house smelled like a stale smoking room in a cheap motel, with gloomy sunlight barely poking through the perfectly pinned curtains. What sort of man pins his curtains closed, Alice wondered? The answer was grim. *A man who has something to hide.*

She wandered through the kitchen into the living room. The house's cavern-like design made it appear larger than it had from the outside. The living room could have accommodated three couches and a dining table, with room for a stupidly suburban entertainment set, yet it only hosted a threadbare couch facing a small TV on a cheap stand, a grand piano against the far wall, and an unadorned fireplace. There were no pictures, no paintings, no mementos; no sign this wasn't a short-term rental. Yet Richard had lived here for over five years.

She whistled nervously as she explored, the soft sound echoing in the emptiness.

Alice turned and headed into the dining room. A display case was filled with china and fine porcelain topped with a thin layer of dust. A small, unpretentious dining table sat in the middle of the room, one chair in front of it. Placed on the table was a laptop computer.

So this was it, she thought. Homestead of M. Martin, world-famous author. Barely an inhabited house, let alone a home.

And then her whistle came back to her, piercing through the silence. Not an echo, but a reply.

Alice froze, every muscle in her body going rigid. And then it came again, floating from somewhere beneath her feet.

"Hello?" she trembled. "Is someone there?"

"Yes, I'm here," a voice, high and reedy, came out of the floorboards. "Are you going to wait up there all day, or come down and see me?"

The door to the basement wasn't locked.

Alice pushed it open and was assaulted by an unbelievably overpowering smell--so sharp she stumbled backwards as if bludgeoned. She coughed, waving her arms about her face, but the odor remained unbearably potent, clinging to her every molecule of her--a pungent combination of sweat, blood and feces.

From deep down within the oppressive void below her came a high-pitched laugh, a cackle so filled with evil her body broke out in sweat.

"Welcome," the reedy voice whispered. "Why don't you come down TO ME."

The last two words roared up out of the blackness and slammed a hook into her. She stumbled forward almost against her will and found herself descending into the darkness of the basement, A darkness which quickly swallowed her whole.

The overpowering stench surrounded her, clinging to the damp walls and curling around the harsh light thrown from the bulbs dangling from wire mounts above her head. In the eerie glow, Alice could make out claw marks gouged into the walls and cement pillars holding up the roof. A pool of almost unnatural darkness huddled around the central pillar of the basement, and out of it peered two feverish yellow eyes.

"Hello, Alice," came the whisper.

She stared at those eyes, twin pools seething with mania, and took an unconscious step forward. Then another.

The creature in the shadows sprang at her faster than humanly possible. One second a pair of eyes glowed in the darkness, the next the unknown entity was fully airborne. Alice barely had time to bubble up a cry of terror as she threw herself to the side. She felt a sharp pain in her shoulder as she landed, then scrambled backward as the creature lunged at her with all its strength, snapping desperately. Bulging veins pierced its pale skin as it strained against a chain-collar wrapped around its neck.

Alice stared directly into hungry, hate-filled eyes as its long, dirty nails clutched the air inches from her face.

In the light, she could tell it was a man, though just barely. It was emaciated nearly to the point of starvation, ribs and cheekbones piercing through his skin. There was no hair atop its angled head, which was covered with bumps and purpling bruises. Claw-like fingernails poked from bony fingers still grabbing and twitching in her direction. Self-inflicted bruises covered its body, mirroring the deep gouges in the wall and pillar, and its tattered clothes held the feral stink of the room.

But it was the eyes that terrified her. Eyes screaming their desire to feed on her pain.

Staring at it, at those eyes, the true danger of the situation fell heavily upon her. "Oh God," she snuffled. "I shouldn't have come." She rose to her feet, eyes locked. "I shouldn't be here."

Abruptly it backed up, staring at her again. "Don't go," it purred, its feral growl turning smooth and silky. "It's been so long since I've entertained guests."

The creature, the mockery of humanity, uncoiled its body--limbs folding around itself. It stood slowly, half in the light and half in the shadows, until it reached its full height of six feet. Then it stepped fully out of the darkness, a completely different entity.

Gone was the snarling, contorted face, the emaciated ribs, the fingers straining for flesh. In its place was a man, arms folded behind his back, legs neatly side by side. He regarded her with a cocked head, even a small, half-smile. But the eyes were the same as before--cold, like a chasm, and sparkling with suppressed fury.

"Alice," His voice rustled gently in her ear. "I've heard so much about you."

She couldn't reply, couldn't so much as move her vocal cords.

"My name is Peter. It's okay, Alice." He sounded calm, even soothing. "Let's talk. I've wanted to speak with you for a quite a while now." Looking almost normal, he regarded her with mischievous eyes. Eyes, she realized with a shock, she recognized. She gasped in stunned disbelief.

"And thus does understanding dawn on the face of the intrepid journalist," Peter chuckled. "My brother might be a fool, but I know why you're really here."

Alice's eyes widened, and his half-smile opened, revealing crimson gums. "You wanted to know." His face filled her vision--the evil eyes, devilish smile, slanted forehead. "So ask. Ask what you came here to ask."

"Why does he keep you down here?" she breathed.

"I'm told I am sick," he said, and the pools under his eyes seemed to deepen till they consumed his hollow face. "And that I cannot be cured."

"Sick?"

He grimaced, and his face suddenly looked pale and sickly. "It runs in the family. Eldest son to eldest son. Which means Dear Richard is, of course, spared. Dad fought our ancestral malady for a while. Tried not to let it consume him. But it just feels so good when it comes on you!"

Peter threw his head back and cackled. The lights in the basement flickered with the shaking of his ribs. He towered above her and she felt a moan rise in her throat.

"Would you like to see?" he whispered.

Abruptly he sprang at her, so suddenly that this time she had nowhere to go. His fingers took root in her hair, yanking her off the ground with brutal strength. Alice cried out as he slung her around, slamming her into him, thrust his snarling face into hers, forcing her to look directly into his cruel eyes.

"I would enjoy this," he said almost intimately. "I would enjoy breaking you."

Alice gasped as the poorly-lit, cement basement melted into something else. Something... horrible. Walls billowed away from her, spires of stone rose from below, light took on a gruesome, violet hue, and her ears were filled with the sound of abject misery. Through all this her eyes remained locked on his, unable to pull away. Unable to even blink. And even as those mad eyes held hers in check, the face around them contorted into a ghoulish nightmare--a vision of pure hunger and madness. No longer a man, her captor's wild smile sliced its jaw in half as its eyes devoured her, shutting out anything she knew to be reality and replacing it with a Hellish construct of its own creation. The concrete floor bucked and slithered, long tendrils shaking themselves out to snake around her wrists and ankles. She strained and struggled, but the ungodly tentacles held her in place. Peter, or the creature that had once been Peter, opened its mouth wide and howled into her face with unbridled desire. Around it, the room screamed back with fiendish delight.

It brushed a strand of hair from her face with an almost delicate gesture. "Welcome to my world, Alice," it whispered. The mad violet glow sparkled in its eyes and she was consumed with a stab of primal fear. "I could consume you right here if I wanted. Right now. You wouldn't be the first."

Abruptly the concrete tendrils relaxed, the walls found solid form again, and the monster before her was no more. It was only Peter. Only a man.

"But I'm not a monster," he cooed, releasing her. "We could help each other. You want a story. The greatest story M. Martin never told. My story."

"And what…" Unadulterated terror caused her to choke on her words. The horrifying vision he had just placed in her mind churned her stomach. How else could he shape her reality? She cleared her throat and tried again. "What do you want?"

Peter captured her gaze once again, and everything around them went dark until the only light available were the two, yellow pinpoints of his eyes. "I want my brother."

Time and space seemed to blur as his eyes bore into her very soul. Alice felt bare beneath his gaze, even violated. "All you have to do is bring him down here. To me. And when the moment is right, give him a little push."

Just like that she was back in the basement, Peter innocently smiling at her. "One little push. And you'll have your story."

Released, Alice ran back up the stairs, out the back door, and over the fence.

His laughter followed her all the way across Pendelwood Court.

"Hey, I live across the street, remember?" Richard Tiwariya said with a friendly smile as she pulled into her own driveway.

"Come inside," she said. "We need to talk."

The entire ride from the airport she'd been unable to look him in the eyes, eyes so similar to the ones chained in his basement. She bolted from the car and marched up the driveway into the house, knowing he was obediently following. Inside, she crossed the living room and took refuge behind the kitchen counter--gripping the edge as a means of staying centered.

Richard came to a stop in the middle of her living room, his face awash in confusion. "What's going on?"

Alice took a shuddering breath to settle her nerves and then dove right in. "I've lied to you, Richard," she admitted, flatly. "I've been lying to you since the day we first met."

A puzzled look came into his face as he subconsciously pulled his head back. "Alice, what are you-"

"I'm a reporter," she said. "I'm with the *New York Post*. That's who I really am." She placed her arm on the counter deliberately, a slow movement that was somehow comforting. "Who you really are is Michael Martin, author of the Sleepy Hollow trilogy."

He started to speak, and she thrust a hand out. "Please. Don't bother."

He crossed his arms, a deep scowl on his face.

"While we're telling truths, I might as well admit that for a while I thought I was falling in love with you," she said, surprising herself with her candor. Even as she said it, she realized it was true. But the time for sentimentality was over. "But now that you know who I am, and I know who you are, we need to talk about what the fuck you're keeping in your basement."

She watched the expressions float across his face, almost in slow motion. First shock, then stunned surprise, followed by rage, ugly and mottled on his weathered face. Then it all wiped away, leaving nothing. Just a dead, empty blankness in his eyes.

She waited for him to respond, the silence stretching into awkwardness. He gave her nothing, just stared sullenly back at her.

"All right, then," she said at last. "I'll take that as a no-comment for tomorrow's front page."

"Wait." Words suddenly spilled out of his mouth. "Don't--please, you can't run a story about this."

She crossed her arms and cocked her head at him. "Then you'd better talk. And then we're going across the street together to talk to your brother."

Richard's breath sucked in. "Alice, you don't realize what you're doing," he said urgently. "You need to leave town immediately. You've met him? Talked to him? Then you're his new prey. You're not safe."

She shook herself. "I can handle myself."

"No, you can't. No one can. Peter is like a cobra, Alice. He entrances his victims. Lures them in." His fingers suddenly tightened on hers, digging painfully into her skin. "The last person he killed was a doctor, who stared right into his eyes as he released his restraints. He does things to your head. Don't let him in."

She faced him, her frown a facade of strength masking her uncertainty. She remembered the other worlds she'd entered down in that basement. The way she'd felt compelled to seek Peter out in the first place. The fluidity of reality in his presence. Don't let him in?

Too late for that.

"Just leave, Alice," Richard was saying. "Just walk away."

If only that were an option. She shook her head. "He wants to kill you. Wants me to help him."

"Are you going to?" he asked.

"I don't want to," she answered.

"You may not have a choice." Richard deflated, as if crushed by an oppressive weight. "I'm sorry."

"Sorry?" she asked, a sinking feeling in her stomach.

"I've seen this before. He's a monster. I should go down there and put a bullet in his head. He begs me to all the time, but I can't. He's my brother. My flesh and blood." He closed his eyes in an attempt to shut out the truth. "You're going back down there. Aren't you?"

And she knew he was right. Though every nerve in her body screamed at her to run, to flee, she knew without a single doubt she was headed back down to that basement. To Him.

"I'll go with you," he said. "You'd force me down there, anyway."

She was horrified to discover he was right yet again.

Alice's eyes watered as they descended the dark basement steps, but Richard showed no sign of even noticing the fetid odor. He drew himself to a stop like an old man as the eyes regarded him from the far corner.

"Hello, Peter," Richard said shakily.

The man-creature rose, bared its teeth at him, revealing a mouth full of sharp, half-rotted teeth. "DON'T CALL ME THAT!" it roared from the darkness.

"This isn't safe," Richard murmured to her. "Please, let's just go."

Alice's jaw moved for several seconds, then she managed to put words out into the thick, stinking air. "Not yet," she stammered. "I want to talk to him."

Abruptly the darkness shifted and Peter emerged, hands behind his back, smiling civilly. He walked pleasantly toward them, the chain around his neck slowly tautening. "A pleasure to see you again, Alice," he drawled. "I trust you are finding the secrets of Sleepy Hollow to your liking?"

"Stop it, Peter," warned Richard, stepping in front of Alice and drawing the kitchen knife he'd brought with him from his waistband.

"Oh, come now, Richard. Allow me my spot of fun. You've brought me a toy." Peter sneered at his brother's feeble weapon and jerked his head forward, inhaling deeply. His sunken nostrils flared as he drank in her scent. "I smell your fear, Alice," he said.

She stared into the eyes, those violent, yellow eyes, and her hand twitched by her side, straining to rise.

"Go on, Alice," said Richard as he stood in front of her, as if to shield herself from his brother's menace. "Ask your questions."

"Yes! Ask me! Ask me anything!" Peter continued. "We have no secrets here. Go on, Alice. Push forward for the truth."

His leering smile widened as Alice's hands rose and opened, placing themselves behind Richard's shoulder blades. She stared at them in horror, unable to stop herself. Her fingers tightened of their own accord. She was no longer in control.

"Please..." she managed to beg, as Peter's face twitched with the effort of quieting the beast within.

Noticing his brother's strain, Richard frowned, "What are you-"

The words exploded in Alice's head.

"GIVE HIM TO ME!"

Alice's arms straightened involuntarily and she leaned forward to shove Richard into the waiting arms of his homicidal brother. In that eager instant, Peter slipped from man to monster.

'Richard, get down!' Alice managed to scream even as her arms jerked forward to shove him to his death.

Richard dropped and Alice's arms shoved against empty air. She stumbled forward even as the monster controlling her pounced, spittle dripping from its jaws, clawed arms outstretched, an expression of fierce joy on its face.

In the span of a heartbeat, Alice accepted death. Her frozen body tumbled into the creature's desperate arms, its claws digging into the flesh of her arms as it caught her with a roar.

"No!" screamed Richard from the floor.

Alice felt sharp teeth press against her throat, but they stopped short of piercing the flesh. The instant of attack over, the creature that was Peter removed his jaws and lifted Alice up in his arms, scowling. "You disgust me," he growled, before tossing her away in disgust.

She slammed into the cold, cement wall and fell to the floor.

Pain exploded in her head from the crack of her skull against the unforgiving wall, and spots momentarily blurred her vision. The world spinning, she rolled onto her side and patted the back of her head, both surprised and confused when her hand came away sticky. The sounds of struggle surrounded her, but it was a moment before she had the presence of mind to look for the source.

Two figures were locked in a vicious embrace, each one screaming, tearing, and clawing with an unrelenting passion. A moment more and Alice's vision cleared enough for her to tell brother from brother. Richard had his hands around Peter's throat, while the elder brother--half man-half monster--had a single claw around his sibling's face, jabbing the other repeatedly into Richard's chest.

Blood from a dozen wounds in his chest pooled at Richard's feet while he kept his hands tight around Peter's throat, staring coolly into his eyes. Another claw thrust and she saw Richard visibly weaken.

"Richard!" she cried in alarm.

Her outburst distracted the monster for the barest of moments, and Richard slammed his brother hard against the central pillar, bringing forth a gasp of shock. "Die!" screamed Richard with glee. "Die! Die! Die!"

His victory was short-lived. The monster in his hands curled both hands into fists and began a torrent of punches directly into the wounds it had already made with its claws. Richard cried out in agony and fell to the ground, Peter falling with him. The monster's fists were red with his brother's blood but the beating didn't stop.

"Alice!" cried Richard. "Help!!!"

Peter, eyes blazing with hatred, slammed a fist into Richard's face to shut him up. Richard's face sagged, his struggles waning.

The knife! cried a voice in Alice's head. *Please, Alice! The knife!*

Alice's eyes widened and she quickly scanned the room, finding the knife resting on the ground near the central pillar. Before her courage had a chance to wilt, she rushed forward, grabbed the knife, spun, and drove it home in Peter's neck.

A font of blood sprayed out, coating her as she withdrew the blade and drove it home a second time. Peter's body spasmed wildly, throwing Alice away, leaving the knife wedged into his neck. He fell to the ground in utter agony, hands reaching up but too weak to reach the blade sending him to his doom.

His head hit the ground with an audible thud, and he turned his dying eyes to Alice, a look of bewilderment on his face--as if unable to believe she had cut him down.

The silence that followed was louder than the brotherly rage that had filled the basement only moments before. Alice stared at Peter's body, still and cruel, and at Richard's body, grasping at straws to remain alive.

"Ri... Richard..." she breathed. "Richard... I..."

"Go," he whispered through clenched teeth. "Run, Alice. Please..."

"But... but you..."

"This is... my..." he closed his eyes and sighed.

"Richard!" she crawled a step toward him, reaching out.

"I'll be fine. Go!" he snapped one last time.

Alice suddenly had to leave. Had to get out of that foul pit of Hell. She scrambled to her feet, her shoes slipping in the blood now covering much of the floor, and ran up the stairs and out of the house.

The bathroom sink was awash in blood.

Alice had managed to get it out from under her fingernails, but try as she might, her hands themselves refused to come clean. She scrubbed her knuckles so much, her own blood began to replace the blood she was trying to wash away. She backed away, leaving the sink a mess. There was simply no way she could deal with any more blood.

Tomorrow. She'd clean it all up tomorrow.

She stripped herself naked upon arriving home and headed straight for the bathroom. Wrapping herself in a towel, she walked over to the fireplace and stared down at the pile of clothes. Waiting to burn. Ready for their fate.

The flame consumed them in seconds.

Unable to eat, she spent the rest of the evening pacing through her living room, chasing away her demons. She wanted desperately to call the police. It was the right thing to do. She'd killed a man. A monster. She should turn herself in.

Yet she hesitated. And continued looking out from behind her closed curtains at the house down the street, waiting for... for what?

For Richard to come back over for dinner on Saturday night like always? To call her up and thank her for a lovely evening? To tell her it had never happened?

She went to bed that night in a daze of fear, shame, confusion, and horror.

Sleep refused to arrive, denying her any escape from her anguish.

She finally got out of bed not long after the sun had risen. Still Richard had not come by, had not called. He hadn't called anyone in--there hadn't been any sirens or flashing lights on Pendelwood Court, so what was he doing? What was going on over there?

Had he died from Peter's attack? Were there two dead bodies lying on the floor of the basement across the street?

Their blood mixing and mingling as it searched for a drain to run down...

Unable to stand it any longer, she quickly got dressed. Before she could think her way out of it, she threw open her front door and marched across Pendelwood Court to the scene of last night's disaster.

"Richard!" she yelled, knocking her bloody knuckles on the front door. "Richard, are you in there? Richard!" She switched from knocking to pounding with her fists, but there was no answer. Fearing the worst, she fled to the back of the house, vaulting herself over the fence once again.

Landing in a crouch, she paused. The house before her looked empty. More than that, it *felt* empty. Alice stood and approached, her heart thumping with the fear of the unknown, the fear of the dreaded, the fear of what lay in wait.

Yet as she stepped onto the worn back porch, her skin did not pucker, her nerves did not twitch. There was no sense of evil emanating from within.

The back door was not only unlocked, but partly open. Alice eased it wide and peered into the gloom of the interior. As the curtains remained drawn, little light crept its way in, despite the rising sun outside.

"Richard?" she called out in a weak voice.

Her steps led her to the basement steps and she peered once again into that tomb of unimaginable horror. After a moment, she pulled out her phone and turned on the flashlight app. The single beam thrust its way down the stairs, an uninvited guest into the oppressive mausoleum. At first her feet refused to follow the beam, but Alice finally managed to lower herself, one step at a time.

Four steps from the bottom, her insignificant dot of illumination alighted on the discolored stonework, dried blood having congealed during the night into a dark mauve.

Three steps from the bottom, she caught sight of withered flesh of an arm splayed out on the ground, the very image of death.

Two steps from the bottom, her phone revealed the former owner of the arm and she cried out in horror, leaping the final stair and dropping to her knees with a wail of misery at the side of Richard's cold corpse.

The knife still deep in his neck.

Right where Alice had left it when she'd thrust it in. Thinking he was his brother.

Peter's chain collar lay open on the floor.

The man, the monster, was gone.

HELL TO PAY
By Amy Bruan

I didn't think anything would go wrong.

The night was perfect. The full moon, the slight autumn chill, the still forest, the infamous bridge, the silent gravestones in the distance, and the Old Dutch Church of Sleepy Hollow watching over me. The pentagram was set and lined with ash, the incense burning, the six black candles lit, my offerings prepared, the book open and ready in my lap. I checked everything. Twice. True, the offerings were a bit unorthodox, but I was pretty sure they'd suffice. I sat on the sidewalk in front of the Headless Horseman's bridge and gathered myself. I figured it would be a perfect summoning spot, since supernatural energy was strong in this area.

At least that was what my mom said.

I bit my lower lip and wondered for the hundredth time if I should have brought Dean with me. He was the prodigal son, after all. Mommy and Daddy's pride and glory, even though he didn't want a damn thing to do with Satanism. Why they kept hounding him on it instead of paying attention to the dutiful son who was actually trying to get their attention was beyond me.

I was the one out here. *I* was the one who would begin a summoning all on my own. *I* was the one who would finally earn their respect. Maybe even their love.

As for what I would do once I had a demon in my back pocket… Well, I'd figure that out later.

I closed my eyes, took a deep breath, and let it out. Then I opened my eyes and read from the old, yellowed pages of the book in my hands. The script was cursive and tightly packed together, making it look almost like chicken scratch. I took another breath and read the first verses in Latin:

Venite ad me sanctus serpens infernorum,
intentator virtuosis ostensor peccatum.
Audite vocem meam,
et gratia apud me obscurum gloria vestra

"Come to me, holy serpent of Hell, tempter of the virtuous, bringer of sin…" The wind began to whip about me as I translated the words into English. I tried shove the flapping corners of the pages out of my mind and concentrate on the writing in front of me.

"I call upon thee, Luci..." I looked around as leaves swirled around my feet. The temperature dropped and I smelled something that reminded me of rotten eggs.

Sulfur, I realized, excited. It was working! But I couldn't see the demon yet.

"Oh! Ah... fer! Lucifer!"

The light of the candles flickered and exploded, igniting the incense. I scooted back from the pentagram, watching with horror and amazement as the flames rushed into the smoke curling up from the incense. The resulting haze glowed a bright orange, stretching until it towered over my hunched frame. Then it widened until a shadow formed inside of it. The shadow reeked of sulfur as it took the shape of a man. I watched the flames curl into his skin and soak into his eyes. He made no scream of pain as he finally formed.

If I didn't know any better, I would swear I'd made a mistake. The guy appeared so... average. Plain brown hair, plain black shirt and blue jeans, plain black boots. He looked like he was in his early twenties, roughly the same age as Dean. His muscles were as big as Dean's too, but he didn't have the same pretty boy looks.

Yeah, if I saw this guy on the street, I would stroll right past him. Until I got a look at his eyes.

They were yellow and slit like a goat's. There was nothing human about them, nothing that could make me doubt who– no, *what*– was standing in front of me.

"Who the fuck are you?" he asked.

I stared, open-mouthed and more than a little impressed with myself. I did it. *I did it.* I summoned a demon! And not just any demon.

I summoned Lucifer, himself!

"Hello? Anybody home?"

I scrambled to my feet, dumping the book on the ground.

"Holy shit! I mean... Wow, holy shit!"

Lucifer rolled his eyes and crossed his arms, glancing at the forest with a bored expression. "Yeah, yeah, good for you, summoning a demon. Mom and Dad will sure be proud."

My heart jumped. "You know about that, Lord Lucifer? You know my parents worship you?"

Lucifer's head snapped in my direction and confusion filled his yellow eyes. "What did you call me?"

Now I was the one confused, I cowed my head slightly, hoping I hadn't somehow just insulted the single most-evil entity in the Universe. "I apologize, oh Dark One. Do you not wish me to call you 'Lord'?"

"Hang on," he said, holding up a plump, uncalloused hand with neatly manicured nails, "Did you just call me *Lucifer*?"

Okay, this is weird... "Would you prefer another name? Maybe Beelzebub, or Belial, or–"

"You think I'm *Lucifer*?"

Dread started to fill my stomach. "Um... you are, aren't you? I mean, Father of Lies, the Deceiver–"

"Sweet Mother Mary and her hidden tits!" burst the demon. "I've been summoned by an idiot!"

"Hey," I shot, "there's no need to be rude–"

"I'm faced with a fucking moron! Did you honestly think you could summon the fucking King of Hell, himself?"

Great. The first demon I summon is a potty-mouthed back-talker. Figures. "Well, then who are you?"

"Lucioafer, dipshit. My name is Lucioafer."

I blinked. He was joking. He *had* to be joking. "Your name isn't really Lucioafer."

Yellow eyes narrowed on me. "You got a problem with my name, take it up with my father. Fucker names all of us bastards after himself."

"You're a bastard of Lucifer?"

Lucioafer rolled his eyes and scoffed. "Look, I'm not here to talk about Daddy issues. Point is, Dad was smart. *No one* can summon Lucifer. He knows how popular he is. All those summoning books you dumb-ass Satanists pray to have been hexed. Anytime someone tries to call him, they screw up the pronunciation and get one of us."

I stared, completely dumbfounded. Was this demon really telling the truth?

"Are we in Sleepy Hollow?"

I glanced around me at the woods, the creepy church, the busy intersection, and the historic bridge spanning the wide creek where I could very easily drown. My summoning location suddenly sucked.

"And it's October, isn't it?"

I whirled around hearing the smile in the demon's voice. Seeing it was worse. Aside from the eyes, Lucioafer looked normal. But the monster showed himself when he smiled. His face split like the Cheshire Cat's, if the Cheshire Cat had two rows of sharp shark teeth. I took a step back, my heart racing in my chest. Lucioafer chuckled.

"Aww, what are you afraid of, Zack?"

"How do you know my name?" I was so scared, I don't know how I got the words out.

Lucioafer's grin widened. "Bastard of Lucifer, remember? I have a trick or two up my sleeve. Mind-reading, shape-shifting, shadow puppets." He dipped his chin, yellow goat eyes gleaming wickedly. "I've always wanted to be the Headless Horseman. He's a righteously evil bastard who knows how to have fun. Think I'll give him a try."

Lucioafer took a step forward. I took three steps back until I remembered he was still in the pentagram. I pointed to it.

"You can't get out! The pentagram is drawn with ash!"

Lucioafer paused and looked down. "So it is. Ash can be good for stopping ghosts." He raised his head, that chilling smile and horrific gaze fixing on me again. "But you know what it's bad for? Stopping demons."

He took a long, exaggerated step... and planted his foot *outside* the pentagram.

I should have started running at that very moment, but the smoke from the incense began to spiral toward his back. Lucioafer held out his hands, the tips of the candlelight stretching to his fingertips. The smoke and fire steadily wrapped around his body. I gagged when the smell of sulfur hit me. Lucioafer's final laugh froze my heart. In an instant he was a pillar of flame and sickly-sweet smoke.

I watched in horror as the pillar took another shape. This one had broader shoulders, something billowing behind its back, and a raised arm gripping a sword nearly as long as me. The head seemed too round and too big for the shape's shoulders.

Finally, the smoke and fire fell away, and I stared at the unholy manifestation before me.

The seven-foot-tall monster had hulking shoulders and bulging arms that strained through his tattered black soldier uniform. A dark cloak dropped to the ankles of his steel-tipped boots. The leather of the boots, as well as of his gloves and vest, had an unnaturally soft look to them, like they'd been made from human skin. In his right hand a gigantic claymore gleamed ominously in the moonlight. A shining beacon illuminating my coming death.

Resting on the stiff collar of the vest was a blazing orange pumpkin with a cruel smile. Flames licked the outside of the carved eyes, nose, and jagged mouth. The exterior of the pumpkin wasn't burning, but the smell could have fooled me.

Lucioafer manifested into the perfect nightmare vision of the Headless Horseman. The flames wafted a couple times, as though a gust of air was pushing them further from his mouth, and I realized he was *laughing* at me.

I turned and bolted. I got three feet before a rough, cold hand fisted the back of my shirt and yanked *hard*. I was a ragdoll in the Horseman's hand, flying through the air until I went over the railing of the bridge. My heels struck the hard ground and I tumbled head over heels down the slope until landing in the creek. I felt the icy chill of the water, the rough smack of the back of my head hitting a rock, then nothing.

I don't know what amazed me more– waking up without water in my lungs, or waking up with my head still attached to my shoulders. Unfortunately, being alive meant being in serious pain. My brain felt like it'd been accosted by an overly enthusiastic heavy metal drummer, and my entire body was frigid from the creek water. I sat up--shivering and soaked to the bone--and quickly looked up at the sidewalk just past the bridge where it entered Sleepy Hollow Cemetery.

The Headless Horseman– Lucioafer– was no longer there.

I crossed my arms, rubbing my hands up and down my biceps to get try and get warm. October nights in New York have no pity for a stupid kid who didn't bring a jacket to his demon summoning.

I was too scared to crawl up the hill again, but I couldn't stay in the water and freeze to death. I shuffled through the creek to the edge of the slope, pressing my chest against the cold earth and scratchy leaves. Digging my hands into the dirt, I crawled up the slope. My body trembled with every motion, my teeth chattering so harshly I thought they would crack. I finally made it to the top of the path and hunched over, hoping I would get more of my body heat back.

The image of the Headless Horseman shot through my head again. I cringed, remembering his massive body, the ease with which he held the sword, the burning smile he aimed at me. A whimper escaped my throat.

Glad as I was to be in one piece, I couldn't help but wonder why Lucioafer didn't kill me. I was easy-pickings, after all. Not a fighter, not good with defensive spells, and apparently easy to throw around.

I craned my neck to look at the trees again. Still no trace of Lucioafer or the Headless Horseman anywhere. Maybe he would hide and catch me when he thought I was safe and relaxed. Though I didn't imagine I was going to be either of those things again.

I would have been happy to lie there and mope, but I had to get home. I had to tell someone what I had done. Meaning I had to talk to Dean and beg him to help me. I didn't see that going well, but big brothers are supposed to help their younger, stupider brothers, right?

Setting my feet against the ground, I pushed to my feet. It hurt to even stretch, the frigidness of my limbs making the slightest twitch agonizing. I curled one arm around my body and used the other to pull my cell phone out of my pocket. Dean was always teasing me for being accident prone, but he'd been thoughtful enough to buy me a reliable cell phone case for my birthday last year.

Thankfully, the phone wasn't damaged. I called him and was monumentally relieved to get his voicemail. I left my message and hung up. He was probably with his girlfriend, Sarah, but he always checked his messages when he saw they were from me. When he heard my message about how I made a huge mistake and almost drowned in freezing water, he would come running. Sarah lived over on Crest next door in Tarrytown. It would take a sane person maybe ten minutes to get here, but I was willing to bet Dean would make it in five when he heard how badly I'd messed up. He'd never pass up a chance to say I told you so.

Sore and cold and counting down the minutes until big brother came to rescue me, I trudged back to the bridge and my summoning kit.

Except it wasn't there anymore.

I went completely still. Everything– the incense, the candles, the offerings, even the book– was gone.

Now I had an idea of what Lucioafer might be up to. But why did he need my stuff? They could only be used by humans.

Right?

I was about to collapse in defeat to the ground when I noticed the light grey ash from my pentagram had been brushed into a new shape. I stared, stepping back to better gauge what I was seeing. It didn't take me long to realize I was looking at words.

Specifically the words, *THANKS, DUFUS.*

No doubt about it--my brother was going to kill me.

"You did *what*?!" Dean roared once we were safely back home and I'd finished the whole humiliating story.

I dropped my head and pulled the edges of the fleece blanket around my shoulders. I wasn't really cold anymore thanks to getting inside and enjoying a soothing mug of hot chocolate, so I was using the blanket more to hide from my big brother's fury than anything else. Dean hadn't been exactly thrilled when I'd explained how Lucioafer had taken on the form of the Headless Horseman and tossed me over the bridge. He hadn't killed me yet, but it was only three in the morning. There was still time.

"I didn't do it on purpose," I muttered.

"You didn't purposefully go to Sleepy Hollow alone the week of Samhain with Mom and Dad's summoning book in the hopes of calling a demon?" he shot back skeptically.

Dean loomed over me as I sat on the edge of his bed. He was twenty-one, five years older than me, and seeing him this angry reminded me of my first sight of Lucioafer. But I took a deep breath and remembered I was looking at my big brother. Tall, broad, and handsome with shiny brown hair, alert brown eyes, and a welcoming smile. Star quarterback, straight-A student, volunteer at the local veterinary clinic where he hoped to work once he finished school. Desperate to get away from his Satanist family roots.

Everything I would never be.

"I didn't mean to summon *that* demon!" I protested.

Dean narrowed his eyes and crossed his arms. I was glad our parents were gone to the local Satanist meeting tonight. I didn't even want to think about what they'd say when they found out I tried to summon the King of Hell and failed. Miserably.

Oh, Zack, Honey. You should have summoned an imp before you called up a bastard of Lucifer. Worked your way up. Summoning Almighty Beelzebub can be tricky.

Yeah. Mom and Dad weren't gonna find out about this. Unless Dean told them, which was still possible considering how mad he was.

"You screwed up, Zack" he snarled. "Cataclysmically screwed up."

I dropped the blanket and put my head in my hands. I may have showered and put on dry clothes, but I still felt dirty and hopeless.

"Look, I know, okay?" I moaned through my fingers. "I knew it the moment he told me his name. I didn't think it was possible to summon a bastard of Lucifer, and I didn't think–"

"No, you didn't think, and that's the whole damn problem! The demon turned into the Headless Horseman, and he's out there somewhere with everything he needs for a demon summoning doing God knows what.

Samhain is two days away, and I'm willing to bet that the reason he took that stuff is because of that night. He's going to do something terrible, and it will put hundreds of people in danger."

Tears pricked my eyes. My chest was tight. I deserved to be chewed out for this, but it hurt coming from Dean. My whole life, I wanted to be as loved as he was. At school, he was the rockstar. I was the skinny weirdo with no friends. He had stellar grades and dreams and a gorgeous girlfriend. I was failing, directionless, and didn't even ping a girl's radar unless I accidentally walked into her.

I should have hated Dean for being better than me... But I couldn't. He was my big brother. He looked out for me when I screwed up, was there for me when I didn't realize I needed help, and never held a grudge against me for very long.

But this was different. This could get innocent people killed. Dean couldn't possibly forgive something like this. He must have been at the end of his rope with me. I couldn't blame him, no matter how much it crushed my soul.

"I know," I whimpered. "I screwed up. You don't have to keep reminding me."

Lucioafer's twisted smile kept running through my head. The same smile that had been on the Headless Horseman's face when he manifested out of smoke and fire. I could still smell the sulfur and burning pumpkin, still see that sword rising in the air, thinking it would come down on my neck and slice off my head. I remembered how strong he had been when he picked me up and threw me off the bridge, and my fear when I realized he could butcher me with in the blink of an eye if he wanted. Just for the fun of it.

I almost jumped out of my skin when Dean settled on the bed beside me. It was a kind gesture, which meant he was probably looking at me with pity. I couldn't decide if that was better or worse than anger.

"Tell me why you did it, Zack. I need to understand."

I turned away. If I told him the truth, it would only make things worse. He already thought I was an idiot. Knowing I was a *jealous* idiot would push him away from me forever. I looked at the door and wondered if I could escape by throwing the blanket over his head and bolting.

Dean's hand curled on my shoulder and squeezed. It was gentle, but I knew he wouldn't let me get away.

"Zack."

I pushed his hand away and shot to my feet, clenching my fists to my sides. It was my turn to shout.

"Because I can't be you, okay?!" I exploded. "I'm useless at school, I don't get the girl, and Mom and Dad don't love me the way they do you! Nobody notices me, and I'm tired of it! I just want to be seen for once! Is that really too much to ask for?!"

Dean stared at me, absorbing all the information I was hurling at him.

"No," he said softly. "It's not. But summoning a demon has never been a good way to get attention."

I slumped and shoved my hands through my hair. I wanted to rip it out by the roots. "It's the only thing I knew how to do."

My brother fell silent. Right then, all I wanted to do was sleep for the next three days. Sleep, and hope that when I woke up everyone in town would still have their heads.

My stomach tied itself in knots. I had no idea how to fix this.

"We have to send him back to Hell," he said.

I sighed. "Yeah, that's obvious, but I don't..." I looked at Dean. "Wait, did you say *we*?"

For the first time that night, Dean smiled at me. I thought I would never see that sight again.

"Of course," he confessed. "Mom and Dad were force-feeding me spells before you could stand. I might not like it, but I do know a thing or two about demons."

"But... But don't you hate me?"

His smile dropped and turned to shock. "Why would I hate you? I'm disappointed and mad as hell, but I don't hate you Zack. You screwed up, but we can fix this." His grin came back. "You can do penance later."

"Thank you, Dean," I whispered, biting my lip.

He waved his hand and pushed himself to his feet. "Don't thank me yet. Part of your penance starts now, with you doing all the dishes by hand for the next three months."

I couldn't suppress my groan. Given how many dishes Mom made for her and Dad's Satanist committees every week, the sink was constantly full of dirty plates, forks, casserole dishes, and sacrificial knives.

But if washing that mountain of grime and grease was the price of stopping Lucioafer from prancing around Sleepy Hollow as the Headless Horseman, it was a price I was happy to pay.

Believe it or not, there are perks to being raised by Satanists. One of them being that when you accidentally summoned the bastard demon-child of Lucifer, you could find information on them pretty easily. We didn't find Lucioafer's name specifically, which even I knew *never* to speak aloud unless I wanted to face him again, but we did find a ton of information on the powers he and his brothers possessed.

Bastard demons usually ended up as imps, little more than slaves for the demons who spawned them. The exception was when they came from Lucifer, the Father of Lies. *His* bastards could change shape, had superior strength, controlled fire, could read minds, and were immortal while in the human realm. Down in Hell, they were basically lowly bike-messengers trying to move up the ranks, sent to answer summonses in place of Lucifer so the big guy could just chill on his dark throne. In truth, they were like anybody else. Desperate for approval from Daddy.

I did not like the obvious, unspoken similarities between Lucioafer and myself in terms of our basic motivations. Particularly when a news bulletin popped up online the next day reading: "THREE FOUND DECAPITATED IN SLEEPY HOLLOW– LONE SURVIVOR RECORDS IMAGE OF HEADLESS HORSEMAN."

This wasn't an article from the local news or a scam paper like Weekly World News, mind you. This was a legitimate article from The Journal News telling me I was seriously screwed.

"Here we go," announced my brother as he walked across the den with an old, dusty book in his hands.

"Please tell me you found something."

He bent at the waist to read the article over my shoulder and read the article, cursing under his breath as I scrolled down to see the image accompanying the story.

The picture had been taken from the parking lot of the Citgo Station on the other side of the Headless Horseman Bridge from where I'd done my brilliant summoning. In front of the bridge lay three bodies, their heads having been removed from their bodies with surgical precision. Looming over the carnage stood a giant black steed with eyes glowing in the camera-phone's dim light. Sitting atop that horse was the Headless Horseman, his mega-creepy pumpkin face turned toward the camera. His right hand held aloft the blood-stained claymore, while his left clutched three blurred-out heads dripping gore onto the concrete.

Evidently Lucioafer was enjoying his new body.

"That's him?" Dean asked.

I swallowed the bile rising in my throat and nodded. Critics would call it a photo-shopped hoax, a teenage prank, a trick of the light, a grainy image. But I knew the image was real.

"The nutcases are going to have a field day," muttered my brother.

I turned in the chair to face him. "You found something, right? Something to stop him?"

Dean nodded and tapped his thumb on his decrepit book. "I don't think these killings are random," he said.

"Why not?"

"Bastard demons want to move up the ranks, right? So how do they gain the approval of their sire?"

I chewed my lower lip, not looking forward to the answer. "A stupidly high body count?"

Dean didn't smile, but his eyes sparkled with humor all the same. "Try again."

I had the answer, but didn't want to think about it. "Please don't make me say it."

"Demons want souls, Zack. The more souls they get, the stronger they become. You don't get a soul just by killing someone." He paced away from the computer a moment, then turned and looked at me, sudden worry on his face. "What did you offer him? When you summoned him? You didn't-"

"Cigarettes and a bottle of Absinthe."

Dean raised his eyebrows. "You raided Dad's booze cabinet?"

"It was that or give him my blood. I'm not a total idiot. I don't want to be a demon's slave for all of eternity."

Giving a demon your blood opens you up to becoming their slave or personal torture toy. And if you gave them your sexual fluids... I shuddered and closed the news article window.

Relieved to learn I had a functioning brain in my skull, Dean relaxed a bit and went back to thinking mode. "Cigarettes and Absinthe. OK. What else does he have? He has candles, which means he has fire," he frowned. "Bastard demons can already control fire, so we have to assume he planning something massive. Something that'll take out hundreds of people who will sell their souls back to him for salvation from the flames."

I agreed. "A really big fire could be enough to nab the attention of..." I paled.

Dean looked at me with wide eyes, having come to the same conclusion. "Daddy."

"But the curse," I argued. "Anyone who tries to summon Lucifer-"

"He's not human," my brother reminded me. "If he tries to summon Lucifer, he won't mispronounce the name. He'll do it."

My brain was overloading from the disastrous possibilities. Not for the first time, I cursed myself for thinking that summoning a demon was a good way to impress my folks. Hell, they weren't even here, this being the week of their all-important Satanist retreat. In fact, I bet they were up there gossiping all about whether these Headless Horseman sightings were real or not with all of their stupid Satanist friends.

Well I wasn't going to tell them.

"We need to trap him," stated Dean. "Effectively."

I frowned. "I can do it."

He tilted his head condescendingly. "Obviously not. I'll set the trap."

"Then what am I going to do?"

"Follow my lead *exactly*. The trap will be much more effective if we put both our energies into it."

"Fine," I grumped. "So when we trap him, what next?"

"We banish the damn thing. Bastard demons are stronger than imps, but an advanced banishing ritual should do the trick."

Should. There was a subjective word if I ever heard one.

Still, much as he might have disliked the truth, Dean was clearly in his element. If he doubted his plan, he was hiding it well. Tomorrow night would see the barrier between worlds at their thinnest. Summonings were always much more effective on Samhain, otherwise known as Halloween. Hopefully banishings were, too.

We had plan. Now we just had to hope like hell that it worked.

You'd think that after three brutal murders, tourists and ghost hunters would do the smart thing and stay away from the Headless Horseman Bridge. You'd be wrong. Despite police cordoning off the intersection, two more people had braved the bridge earlier that day.

Two more people had lost their heads.

I didn't know what Lucioafer was doing with the five souls he'd collected so far. Maybe he had a plan or maybe decapitation was just his way of passing time while waiting for the big night. Whatever the reason, he was a bloodthirsty lout. Heading into this, I was about as excited as a mouse approaching a starving lion's den.

The night got off to a bad start when we parked illegally along Broadway just outside of Philipsburg Manor, walked south past the Old Dutch Church to the ill-fated intersection, and found the Bridge *packed* with tourists. Even though it was one in the morning, a hundred people stood milling about in the driveway to the Old Dutch Church on one side of the bridge, and a hundred more in the Citgo parking lot on the other side. The harried police were doing all they could to keep folks away, but it was a lost cause.

At least two paranormal "experts" shouted to their respective groups about the history of the town, the legend of the Horseman, and the significance of Samhain. A line of four uniformed police officers stood in a semi-circle across the bridge, just off the curb, with hands on their belts. A last line of defense in case someone tried to run forward onto the bridge and contaminate the crime scene just to be closer to true darkness of the scene.

I doubted that would make a difference once Lucioafer showed up in his fancy costume.

"This is a disaster," Dean muttered angrily from where we stood by the church behind the crowd. "Even if he reaches the bridge, we won't have time to put the circle together."

"No," I agreed. "Not unless we can draw him over here into the Old Dutch Burial Ground and then run back to the bridge to quickly make the circle."

Dean frowned. The harvest moon waning over our heads cast an aggressive shadow across his intimidating face.

"That'd be cutting it close," he said.

"We've spent the last two days practicing," I countered. "We can do this."

He was torn. Leading the Headless Horseman/Lucioafer through a crowd of innocent people was dishonorable and would more than likely cost lives. But doing nothing would undoubtedly cost a lot more. He knew I was going through with this, with or without his help. He also knew I'd never succeed alone. I wasn't giving him much choice.

But I didn't care. Five people were dead because of me, their souls trapped and enduring God knew what at the hands of a monster of my creation. Hundreds more would suffer the same fate if we didn't stop it. I *had* to make this right.

My brother read my face and saw my resolve. It bothered the hell out of him, but he slumped his shoulders and let out a nervous sigh.

"Alright," he complied. "We'll do it your way."

I nodded. We stood at the edge of the bustling crowd, staring across the bridge, one of us grumpy, the other ready to crap his pants.

An hour must have passed before the wind around us picked up, swirling dead leaves in a vortex of ceaseless doom.

The crowd fell into quiet murmurs, all heads turning toward the stone bridge. A thick black cloud smothered the harvest moon, casting everyone in shadow. Murmurs became whispers. Dean walked through the crowd to get a better view. I followed, ducking my head and praying Lucioafer wouldn't catch sight of me in the crowd. If he spotted me, our plan was shot.

Calm down, I told myself as the temperature plummeted. *Calm down, focus on the plan, do it right. You've got Dean this time, you...*

A trail of fog drifted up from the creek below to waft over the bridge. Everyone took a step back. Even Dean.

The paranormal experts raised their voices to try and calm everyone down, telling everyone this was just part of the supernatural magic of Samhain. The cops tried to report in over their radios, but were met with static. The crowd inched away nervously from the display. It was showtime. Dean and I stared towards the bridge as the fog lifted into the air and became a wall.

The scent of the fog was strange. I sniffed a couple times, then looked at Dean, who nodded. Incense. Lucioafer was making the most of the kit I'd inadvertently left for him.

A woman gasped. Heads turned. An orange glow came from inside the wall of smoke. Next, a dark shadow began to take shape. The crowd was on the verge of panic. Fear shot into my heart as the shadow formed into the shape of a massive horse topped by a gigantic man sporting a burning pumpkin atop his shoulders.

And then the Headless Horseman stepped out from behind his wall of fog. Some people gasped, others screamed, one fainted. All stared in rapt fascination as this impossible display of Legend came to life in front of their eyes. The demonic rider violently jerked his horse to the side, displaying his grotesque collection of human heads dangling beneath the saddle. Now everybody screamed, but no one could bring themselves to move or turn away.

The Horseman kicked his horse forward a step with a sharp whip of the reins, drawing an angry scream from the jet black beast.

"It's alright, everyone," one of the paranormal 'experts' standing in the driveway of The Old Dutch Church called out in a shaky voice. "Legend says the Horseman can't cross to this side of the bridge because of the church. Only those on the other side have to run from him. We're perfectly safe."

This caused quite a few of the folks in the Citgo parking lot to scatter, but the Horseman ignored them, remaining focused on this side of the bridge. My side. Something told me he'd heard the man's announcement. I could all but see Lucioafer's smile behind that burning pumpkin face. He must have been waiting for the invitation, because he kicked the horse's flanks and bolted forward.

Chaos erupted as the Horseman charged across the bridge towards the church. People scattered, some running for the church, others running into the burial ground surrounding it. Some people just ran blindly through the intersection without direction. The cops stood their ground, pulling their guns and firing every shot they had at the advancing menace.

The bullets struck the Horseman's chest to no effect, with some of them even ricocheting off his grinning pumpkin face. He didn't slow down as he closed distance and drew the claymore from the scabbard at his side. The cops gave up and ran.

Dean grabbed my arm and pulled me toward the creek as soon as the Horseman had crossed over it. Terrified screams cut through the night, silenced by a slashing blade. I forced myself not to turn around.

We vaulted the rusty iron fence and slid down into the stream. The water was as cold as I remembered, but I didn't slow down. In less than a minute we were across and back up the opposite bank. Dean threw himself over the fence and raced to the far end of the bridge, dropping to his knees. He tossed the backpack on his shoulders to the ground and ripped open the zippers. I fell to my hands and knees at his side and together we rummaged through the pack, brought out the vials of holy oil we'd stolen from our folks' cupboard--along with a canister of salt--and began drawing a circled pentagram. If we did everything right, Lucioafer would be contained within long enough for us to banish him. We worked fast and concentrated as hard as we could. Creating the pentagram in a rush was dangerous, the sigils had to be exact. But I had my focus this time. I'd practiced this with Dean over and over again the past two days until the work was more muscle memory than coherent thought.

"Done," I announced.

"On the last one," Dean replied, sprinkling salt onto the last sigil.

I lifted my head and looked across the bridge towards the Old Dutch Church to see how things were going.

One of the cops lay on the pavement, his brave attempt at a last stand having cost him his head. The Horseman stood over him, his bloody sword in one hand and the severed head in the other. As I watched in horrific fascination, the towering form of blackness tied the poor cop's head to his saddle, adding it to his collection. Once that was complete, he straightened up and looked towards the church. Inside, a massive crowd had taken sanctuary and now watched this figment of nightmare through the windows. Upon seeing the Headless Horseman survey the church, the survivors within screamed as one. Grinning, the Horseman grabbed the horse's saddle and swung himself up. He pivoted, ready to charge forth, but suddenly came to an abrupt stop.

He slowly turned his head, far more than any head should have been able to turn, until his flaming pumpkin eyes locked onto mine.

"*You!*" I heard him scream in my head.

I grimaced and clutched my ears as Lucioafer's voice bounced through my skull. Dean said my name, but I could barely hear him. I slowly dropped my hands and looked up. The Horseman was charging our way, faster than before.

Dean grabbed my elbow and pulled me to my feet. He stood beside me, ready to defend me like all big brothers feel compelled to do.

"*You brought your brother,*" Lucioafer echoed. Every word was a nail pounding into my brain. "*Good. I want to see your face when I take his head and catch his soul. He looks strong. I can't wait to give him to my father.*"

There was no way I could protect both of us from Lucioafer. One swing of that sword, and it would be over.

The Horseman bounded closer, his horse's hooves pounding thunderously. Flames streaked around the pumpkin head and severed heads bounced against the horse's flank below him. He raised the claymore high as he crossed the bridge. It was all I could do to hold my ground.

When the demon was mere feet from the circle, Dean shoved me to the side as hard as he could. I felt more than saw the sword come down, and heard a loud *thunk* as I landed face first on the ground. Something heavy dropped beside me. I coughed and rolled onto my back in horror.

Dean lay motionless in the dirt beside me. With a burst of terror, I shot my hand out and felt for his neck, praying to any deity that would listen for a miracle.

My prayers were answered. Dean's neck had not been severed. He still had his head. His hair was matted with blood and I realized he must have been hit with the hilt of the sword when he pushed me out of the way.

The crazy scream of the unearthly beast behind me jolted me to my feet. There, against all odds, sat the Headless Horseman atop his steed, trapped in our pentagram and waving his sword furiously through the air. Flames poured forth from his eyes and mouth.

"*You little shit!*" Lucioafer screeched in my head.

I gritted my teeth against the stabbing pain in my head, but didn't lose my ground.

"*Heed my words, spawn of Hell. You stand in a holy circle blessed with the sigils of angels, and I tell you that you are not welcome here. You are banned from this plane, demon Lucioafer,*" I commanded with the Latin phrase Dean and I had drilled into our heads the past two days.

The Horseman jerked in his saddle like he was being electrocuted. His tremors became so violent that he finally fell from his saddle onto the ground. It's connection with the demon severed, the fire in the horse's eyes faded back to normal, and the poor creature bolted from the circle and across the street into Philipsburg Manor.

Slowly, the Horseman rose to his feet, the fire in his own eyes beginning to dim from rage red to a more sedate magenta. The haze of incense smoke wrapped around him once again and he immolated into a pillar of flame and smoke. Within that inferno, his shape altered, shifted, and settled. When the smoke and fire dissipated, I was staring at the yellow-eyed human form of Lucioafer. An ugly snarl curled his lips, revealing the sharp teeth I had once feared.

"Asshole," Lucioafer growled. "I haven't had this much fun since Dad let us re-enact Sodom and Gomorrah in our basement!"

I folded my arms over my chest, ignoring the revelation that Hell had a basement. "Tough. You're going back to Hell."

Lucioafer rolled his eyes. "You summoned me because you wanted to impress your folks, who clearly love pretty boy over there," he nodded to Dean. I wanted to check on my brother, but I didn't dare avert my eyes from the demon. "You really gonna blame me when I was just trying to do the same thing?"

"I didn't kill anyone."

He snorted. "Keep telling yourself that. Those deaths are on your conscience. If you hadn't tried to be a show-off and summon Lucifer, then–"

"Heed my words, spawn of Hell. You stand in a holy circle blessed with the sigils of angels, and I tell you that you are not welcome here. You are banned from this plane," I droned in Latin once again.

Lucioafer winced. He was getting very uncomfortable in the circle.

"All right. Shit, you made your point, just–"

"Heed my words, spawn of Hell. You stand in a holy circle blessed with the sigils of angels, and I tell you that you are not welcome here. You are banished from this plane."

The demon started panting and sweating. Fire burst forth at the edges of the circle and worked its way inward toward his feet.

"Zack, listen to me. You can't do this. My dad will kill me when he sees how seriously I failed up here. You don't know what he'll do to me–"

"Heed my words, spawn of Hell. You stand in a holy circle blessed with the sigils of angels, and I tell you that you are not welcome here. You are banished from this plane. Begone forever."

"Christ, give it a rest, will you?" Lucioafer convulsed and dropped to his knees, screaming as his hands fell into the flames. I flinched and stepped back, part of me feeling bad about what I was sending him back to. The guilt stopped when I considered the six severed heads still hanging from the side of a now very-spooked horse somewhere in the Manor.

The flames curled around Lucioafer until they consumed him completely. He threw back his head and howled and I watched the last of his body disappear into the fire. The entire blaze shimmered once, then vanished into thin air, leaving behind nothing but a smoking pentagram and the faint smell of sulfur.

I let out the breath I hadn't known I'd been holding, my relief like a physical weight being lifted from my shoulders. I'd done it. Lucioafer was gone.

Whirling around, I rushed to Dean's side, dropped to my knees, grabbed his shoulders, and shook him more roughly than was probably necessary.

It worked, though. I heard his quiet groan and saw his hands move to the side of his ribs. I helped him sit up slowly. The last thing my brother needed right now was a headrush.

He sighed and put a hand on the back of his head, pulling it away to find blood. Frowning, he looked over his shoulder at the smoking pentagram, then at me.

"Did you banish the bastard all by yourself?"

I nodded. "Seeing you get smacked in the head kinda set me off and I didn't want to wait for you come around." I smiled hesitantly. "Not bad, right?"

Not bad? Six people were dead because of my foolishness. Which, truth be told, was pretty damned bad. But I couldn't think about that now. Later I'd feel guilty. Now I was awash with relief that my brother was alive.

"Not bad," Dean said, smiling gently. There was some sadness in his eyes. I could see he was blaming himself for the cop as much as I was. At least I wouldn't have to carry the entire burden alone.

Dean clapped me on the shoulder and gave me a brotherly shake. "I take it you learned your lesson?"

"Yeah. Never summon a demon without speaking their name properly."

"Zack."

"I'm kidding, okay? Never summon a demon. Ever, ever, ever."

Dean smiled. "Much better." He looked across the bridge, and his smile changed. "Looks like you picked up some fans."

"Huh?"

I followed my brother's line of sight and watched about a hundred dazed survivors pour out of the church. Who knew what they'd seen or heard from inside, but their eyes were filled with gratitude.

They were looking at me, really looking at me.

I didn't think they were going to forget me any time soon.

THE DYING DREAM OF MAJOR ANDRE

By Robert Stava

"**S**o is the story true or not?" Sheila Gozigian asked me with just a touch of a slur in her voice.

"Of *course* not, it's complete rubbish." I answered, perhaps a little too quickly.

She looked sharp in the shimmering cocktail dress, with the low cut back and dipping bust-line that emphasized her cleavage. Sheila was one of the better-known local realtors – if you didn't catch her charming smile from her weekly ad in the Gazette you'd probably catch it looking up at you from the paper placemat ads at one of the local diners. She was sort of relentless, but also quite sexy in a bold sort of way with her intense eyes, Mediterranean complexion, and appealing figure.

Her question was about the picture, of course, one that had come into my collection a couple weeks previous and was scheduled to go up for auction sometime after the first of the year. It had been quite the buzz around town this Christmas season, a previously unknown sketch by that ill-fated British officer of the American Revolution, Major John André.

'The Dying Dream of Major André' it was being called; a dark, somewhat disturbing pen drawing he had made of himself . . . and of the nightmare that had allegedly visited him shortly after being captured and imprisoned as a spy. Not the better known self-portrait he did, currently in the Yale library. That one shows a sad, introspective version of Andre sitting at a table in a resigned pose, contemplating his fate. No, this one was a more hastily drawn image, more haunting . . . almost *insidious* in its immediacy.

Certainly it was a fantastical idea--this leering, horrific she-creature he sketched into his prison chamber next to him . . . .

"Obviously it was some sort of bad nightmare or premonition he had after he'd been captured," I added, taking a nervous pull off my brandy. I'd been having strange dreams about the painting since it had come into my possession. "Perfectly understandable given his circumstances, I would think."

Christ I sound like such a horse's ass sometimes, I thought, enjoying the inviting view of Sheila's bosom.

It was my third Christmas party in two weeks and I was already on the verge of burnout. This one was the biggie in the Wyvern Falls' Historical Society's calendar however: the annual gala dinner and silent auction held at the Sleepy Hollow Country Club. Which worked out rather well, I thought; the sprawling English-style estate was beautifully decked out for the season, its rolling lawns overlooking the Hudson picturesque under a light covering of snow.

The silent auction was over and I'd run into Sheila in the front library, browsing over the club's display cases featuring a cross-section of antique photos and artifacts from the club's glory days. Most of the images featured Vanderlips and Rockefellers, though I'd heard the club had been built with Vanderbilt money.

"His capture?" Sheila asked, one eyebrow arching up. I had her pegged at late thirties – a really *good* late thirties in her case. She was one of those women who grew sexier with maturity. Though perhaps a little too aggressive for my tastes.

"Yes. His capture. You *do* know the story, don't you?"

"Well . . . yes," she said hesitantly.

Clearly she didn't. Like most people, she was probably only focused on the more sensationalistic rumors surrounding the drawing: that it was cursed, and that it was somehow connected to two recent, grisly deaths.

Normally I would have dropped straight into professorial mode and started lecturing, but – perhaps it was just the brandy – I thought I detected a hint of (sexual?) interest on her part and held my tongue. It might have been my imagination, but I could have sworn she moved an inch or two closer. Enough to get a decent whiff of her perfume, which was something subtle and rich like Nina Ricci.

"Would you like to hear it?" I asked as we strolled over toward the fireplace. The remaining dinner-goers were still in the main dining room or in the old billiard room, which tonight served as the main bar.

Sheila swirled her champagne flute and tilted her head, a light smile on her face. "That depends . . . is it a good story?"

I placed one hand on the mantel piece and, glancing up at the coat of arms carved in its wood, shrugged, "It's a rather tragic one, I'm afraid," trying to sound bravely nonchalant, "Not necessarily a good sentimental Christmas tale."

"Oh, I've had it up to the gills with Christmas tales . . . and flat housing sales. After this past week, a good tragedy would cheer me up!"

"Well, don't say I didn't warn you." I glanced around the room, gathering my thoughts. The library exuded the stuffy charm of well-used, old money – elaborately carved wood paneling and the lofty, ornately detailed plaster ceiling one finds in homes of only the truly rich. The room was dominated by the fireplace, which looked like it belonged in an English mansion. A fire snapped and crackled in the grate; with the high-backed leather chairs, bookcases, and wall-hung oil paintings darkened with age, the entire room might have been snatched out of a Dickens novel. Especially with the antique-looking Christmas decorations and frost-tinged windows.

An excellent room for a story in other words.

"I understand he was quite a likable fellow," I began, "The Major was a gentleman, handsome, well-mannered . . . a man of honesty and integrity. Bit of a dandy, really. The tale almost runs like a black comedy. And so it might have been if it hadn't ended so sadly. It all started with Benedict Arnold. I'm sure you've heard of him."

"The traitor?"

"The very one. Of course, before he became a turncoat, Arnold was one of Washington's more successful Generals– most people forget that. A bit of a rock star in his time, he was a man known for his bold and daring tactics, winning several crucial victories early in the Revolution. Unfortunately, his ego grew faster than his pocketbook. Eventually his excessive lifestyle, along with seeing several lesser officers get promoted over him, got the better of him. Arnold sought and was awarded command of West Point--an impenetrable fortress whose deadly cannons ensured British forces would be unable to journey up the Hudson into Continental territory--and prepared to hand it over to the British for the princely sum of twenty thousand pounds--about $1.2 million in today's dollars. We'll never know for certain, but had he succeeded, it might have ended the Revolution then and there."

Sensing her attention starting to wander at this point, I picked up the pace and spiced up the facts a little. "Er, so one late September day in 1780 Major André was sent up the Hudson in a British sloop-of-war, the HMS Vulture, with orders to rendezvous with Arnold and procure from him critical information about West Point. But things started to go right into the toilet from the get-go.

"The Vulture came under fire after dropping Andre off at Haverstraw and was forced to retreat downriver, stranding André in enemy territory. Faced with the proposition of sneaking back through enemy lines in broad daylight, Andre ditched his uniform and set out to return to White Plains in disguise.

"About a half mile north of Tarrytown – near Philipsburg Manor actually – three American Volunteers stepped out and stopped him at gun-point. Seeing one of the men wearing the coat of a Hessian soldier--allies of the British-- André told them he was a British officer. When they revealed they were actually American, André abruptly switched his story, trying to convince them he was actually an American as well, producing as evidence a bogus travel pass provided him by General Arnold. They didn't buy it, and took Andre prisoner.

"He was delivered to Continental forces and promptly began an absurdly comical journey of being marched from one outpost to another and often back again. At one point, he was actually sent to – of all the damndest people – *Benedict Arnold* up at West Point. Unfortunately for Andre, his party was recalled before he reached his co-conspirator."

I paused to take a healthy swig of my brandy. "Still with me?" I asked.

Sheila sipped her champagne and, holding it up to see there was still a third of a glass left, nodded. "I'm good. Keep going."

"Humiliating as it was, André maintained his composure throughout his ordeal. He was eventually convicted for being a spy and sentenced to the gallows. And late in the morning of October 2nd, Major John André was loaded into a wagon and driven to a 'hanging tree' on a hill just outside of Tappan, New York. At the stroke of noon the wagon was rolled forward, leaving poor André to choke out his last like an animal. Twenty or so minutes later the Major's lifeless body – in full dress uniform – was cut down and buried in a crude coffin below the gallows . . . ."

Sheila let out a shudder and drained the glass of champagne just as one of the caterers materialized with a tray of freshly poured glasses. With the grace of a seasoned pro she swapped out her empty and took a healthy gulp.

"Cheers," I said, clicking her glass with my brandy. "Which brings us to the crux of the tale – the drawing, or rather, the *secret* drawing."

Sheila seemed to edge in a little closer again. There was no doubt at this point she wasn't just interested in a little bed-time story. *But why not?* I thought; *I'm single, in good physical shape for a 46-year-old guy, and reasonably well-off.* And though maybe it was the alcohol doing some of the talking, there was no denying she was attractive. There was that single-parent thing, and that aggressive "cougar" reputation of course, but I didn't think anyone would think much the less of me if we happened to hook up. But there was something else there too, something oddly compelling about her that made me just a little nervous . . .

"The *secret* drawing?" Sheila prompted. "What's so secret about it?" Reaching out she touched my hand with her finger in a light caress – a seemingly careless gesture that was somehow erotically charged. I felt goosebumps break out along my arm, and an answering twinge below the waistline.

"Er, yes. Well it came as a bit of a surprise when it surfaced this past year. In the attic of an old house up in Schenectady. It was discovered purely by chance in the backing of an antique mirror dating from the mid-1800s – the person in question was attempting to replace the glass – and the first response was that it was some sort of hoax. I mean a 'secret' drawing by Major André? And a nightmarish one at that? It didn't make sense. There'd never been a suggestion such a thing existed before, and the very nature of it seemed inconsistent with the Major's character. Which was where I was called in."

Here I straightened my back and made that little rise of the eyebrow I'd perfected from years of art dealing. From her rapt expression it appeared that I had her undivided attention. As to who was hooking whom, well that was another matter.

"It wasn't until a few other pieces of the puzzle came to light that it all began to make sense," I continued. "The house, it turned out, was owned by a descendant of David Williams – one of the three militiamen who captured the Major on that fateful September day. But it was the journal excerpt that I turned up in the State Archives in Albany that clinched it. Do you believe in 'Divine Provenance'?"

"Do you mean 'Providence'?" She answered.

She's even sharper than I guessed, I thought. "No, 'Provenance', as in the way some items will themselves to be revealed or discovered at the necessary time. While researching some papers up in Albany I found a journal fragment from David Williams, himself, explaining how he was given this drawing from Major André, himself.

"Now the thing about this drawing is that it shows the Major slumped in what appears to be a sort of prison cell. At first it appears he's weeping or distressed, but looking closer it's more apparent he's cringing in terror. That's no doubt due to the other figure in the drawing, a nightmare succubus straddling his legs. She's partially nude, revealing her pubic area no less (an unheard of detail for that time period) along with one ample breast. But it is her hideous face that grabs the eye. Half ravishing beauty, half leering demon; with one claw-like hand clutching at the area over his heart. Her hair is sprayed out as if in a gust of wind, and her feet have erupted into the scaly talons of a raptor. The whole thing has a horrid, lifelike energy to it . . . like that of something drawn from first-hand observation. And there's a caption: 'The Dying Dream of Major André – a most horrid Death is upon me.' But here's the catch; the drawing was apparently made by André, himself . . . about a *week* before he was executed."

"I don't understand," Sheila replied, not quite convincingly.

"According to the journal scrap, which I have reason now to believe was deliberately buried due to its controversial (and supernatural) implications, André surrendered the drawing to Williams the morning after he was first captured. Williams took it from André as he was about to destroy it, thinking it might be a secret message of sorts. André was of course mortified, and said something strange; 'I thought it odd Lady Shippen should visit me last night . . . but then . . . oh God! What was it? I am damned and death is upon me . . . no good shall come of this . . .' First he begged Williams to burn it, then implored him never to show it to anyone, making him swear upon his honor.

"For whatever reason, Williams agreed. The drawing disappeared from the world . . . for a time at least. According to family records, the drawing turned up again, twice, during the eighteen-hundreds. Harold Falk posited that the first appearance was in—"

"*Falk?*" Sheila interrupted, "Wasn't he one of the two men they just found dead?"

"Er, yes, he was the art scholar originally hired to confirm the provenance of the piece . . ."

"It was awful, though!" Sheila plowed ahead, "The papers said . . ."

"Yes-yes," I cut in before she could go any further. I knew what the papers had said, of course, but they didn't begin to tell the gruesome story. *I* was the one who had discovered Falk's body, along with the corpse of his landlord. Instantly the terrible images sprang to mind: Falk's fish-white naked corpse sprawled amongst the bedsheets, his face a snarling rictus of terror. And the wounds . . . like he had been mauled by . . . a tiger? Blood had been spattered everywhere, even on the ceiling. Most of the landlord had been found on the attic stairs. It appeared as if she had been trying to escape.

I sensed the moment was slipping somewhat and hastened to wrap it up. "So, er, apparently there were a couple of additional incidents . . . and deaths attributed to the drawing in the 1800s that the family kept out of the news. A great-grandson of David Williams – a man named Jeremiah Watkins – was asked to destroy the drawing. But being a print-shop owner and art enthusiast he decided not to and concealed the drawing in the mirror instead, where it lay hidden and forgotten until last year when it turned up quite by chance."

At this point I was standing with my arm extended, hand resting on top of the fireplace mantel, and was aware the other partygoers had left the library at some point, leaving just the two of us. Sheila smiled and leaned into my arm. If I had any doubts about her intentions before, I certainly didn't then.

How long since I'd been with a woman? Still, I had to tread carefully. Sheila had a young daughter at home, I reminded myself.

But there was something else going on as well, completely non-sexual believe it or not; part of me was uncomfortable about spending another night alone in my bed. Especially after the nightmares I'd begun having the past few nights . . .

"Would you um . . . would you like to . . . ?"

Sheila smiled, her face now only inches from my own. I was aware again of her perfume and how much I missed a woman's intimacy.

"Yes . . . let's get out of here!" she suggested.

Outside it was a crisp, clear December night, the kind where every constellation in the universe seems to have been thrown across the heavens in frozen relief. Just past the belt of Orion came the blink of a passing jet ferrying its unknown passengers across the frigid skies. To the west, the Hudson River Valley sprawled in a majestic winter panorama. Through the barren trees came the crystalline wink of lights from across the river, the warmer ones hinting at cozy households bundled up against the darkness.

Sheila linked her arm through mine as we walked toward the few remaining vehicles parked around at the back.

The dinner had been winding down to a drunken ruckus in the club's 'Morning Room' where I'd said goodnight and a hearty thanks to the Historical Society president, Wes Fowler and Jack Underhill, the vice-president. Fowler was also the captain on the 'Falls Police Department while Underhill was from old local money and had a colorful reputation as a bit of a hell-raiser. Underhill had clapped me on the back as I'd turned to escort Sheila out and given me a knowing wink.

"What did you have in mind?" Sheila asked, huddling close. Despite the heavy coat, her legs--in high-heels and sheer stockings--must have been freezing.

"How soon do you need to get home?" I asked in return.

"Sunday." She answered. "My ex has my daughter until then." She must have sensed my alarm as she quickly added, "Oh, don't worry, I'll be out of your hair well before that! I promise."

I laughed as we drew up in front of her car, which was a surprise as it was a Subaru. Somehow I'd pictured something flashier, like a Cadillac SUV or a sports car.

"What do you say I lure you back to my place, fix up a little fire and a nightcap? It's not all that far up the road."

"Do you have champagne?"

"I'm sure I could rummage something up." I replied, mentally kicking myself; *"Rummage up?" Good Christ, why do I keep talking like such a stuffed shirt?*

Sheila didn't seem to notice. Instead she snuggled in closer.

"I'll follow," she giggled.

I had no idea what time it was when I snapped awake, only that it was in those cold twilight hours long before dawn when the world is awash in shades of despair and darkness.

The dream had been terrible: I had been sitting in a rustic, low-ceilinged room, where someone was sobbing. Grey light was coming through a small, thick-paned window. The heady, cloying odors of hay and animals . . . and something else. The coppery aroma of fear. And grief. The certainty that all life's machinations, dreams, and desires are about to drop down a chute into eternal nothingness, the flat horizonless gulf of death. I was looking down at my hand resting on the rough-hewn table, marveling at the heavy cuff of my jacket with its tarnished brass buttons; the soiled linen of the shirt sleeve peeking out and the quill pen lying slack in my fingers . . . and the drawing. And then not wanting to but forced – as if by unseen controls – to slowly turn my gaze upwards toward the form floating by the ceiling, already seeing the hovering nightmare banshee--half erotic woman, half-skeletal demoness--with its rippling gown trailing in tatters around it. It was like some awful materialization of my worst fears emerging through the gossamer web of reality . . .

It took a few moments for my senses to assemble themselves into some sort of sensible order of the present; the weight of someone straddling my lower body, the cool draft from the dark shadows of my bedroom, the shivering tingle of sweat evaporating off my brow and chest. The moon must have risen – from the window next to my bed the glow revealed the sensuous curves of a woman's breasts. And movement, the suggestion that her head – bathed in shadow – was surrounded by a cloud of floating hair like sea grass caught in an ocean tide.

Of course!

Sheila!

So! She'd warmed up for a little 'action' after all!

It came back to me in a flash . . . pulling into the driveway of my converted carriage-house by the river . . . the scintillating sparkle of snowflakes (from the previous day's dusting) blowing off the tree limbs in the glow of the outdoor sensor light triggered as we stepped up to the front porch. Quickly setting a fire in the fireplace in the cozy, dark-paneled front room, surrounded by some of my more favorite antique paintings and art pieces. Nacho, my over-sized Norwegian Forest cat, wandering in and giving Sheila a dismissive once-over before settling down into his favorite spot on the ottoman. The pop of the champagne cork (a vintage bottle of Krug I'd been saving) and the light reassuring fizz as the glasses were filled. Standing by the fire, then, on an impulse, turning about, bending over Sheila on the couch and the awkward moment as I tried to kiss her on the lips and she'd turned away.

"I'm sorry," she'd said. "It's just . . . I know I acted a little forward earlier . . . but I recently got out of a divorce . . . could we just enjoy each other's company a bit?"

Embarrassed, I'd let out a short laugh to cover my disappointment. "Sorry, that *was* a little presumptuous of me. Of course. It's a nice night to enjoy a fire . . ."

We stayed like that a bit, drinking, then at some point we did go up to bed, got half-undressed and snuggled up. I remembered I'd lain there a few minutes, listening to the wind picking up outside, the trees creaking and the keening moan as it whipped along the gutters and eaves. Sometime later, while savoring the low banked heat of her body next to mine I drifted off into the deeper waters of sleep.

Then I came to . . . for a little bonus surprise to the evening after all.

Outside I could still hear the wind whipping around the house and trees and had a lingering thought about how fortunate it was to be in warm bed on such a hostile winter night.

At first I started to smile, thinking. *There are worse things in life than waking up to find a sexually aroused woman straddling you on a cold December evening* . . . before realizing something was wrong. Terribly wrong. As she leaned forward the moonlight revealed her face.

I screamed.

Or at least tried to. It seemed to get all trapped and snarled in my mouth and came out as more of a garbled choke.

It still looked like Sheila . . . somewhat. The face was a distorted--decayed actually--caricature with skin the color of moldering lace, and blackened fangs through which issued a faint mist, as if the thing's breath was of icy fumes of a winter grave. Then the smell hit me, equally horrific; of things long dead and putrefied.

I tried to pull myself backwards but found I was already up against the headboard. And the thighs gripping my hips felt as immovable as iron.

The head extended towards me, the jaws beginning to open with a hideous creak as I was embraced by numbing cold, when to my further shock the door to the hallway was thrown open and the creature was suddenly cast in a yellow light.

It was Sheila--or rather, the Sheila I had picked up at the party. She stood in the doorway wearing my bathrobe, a wide-eyed look on her face. The... thing... straddling me snapping its head toward her and hissed like an enraged lizard. A throttled scream finally escaped past my lips.

The surprises weren't over yet, however.

Scarcely missing a beat, the real Sheila snarled back at the creature with a cry of "You bitch!" while grabbing the nearest thing she could reach--one of my antique, mission-style floor lamps. Even as the creature in my bed launched itself at her, it was met with a sickening crunch as the cast iron stand was swung around like an unwieldy quarterstaff. I winced as the stained glass shade shattered, as much from the sheer violence of it as from the loss of an invaluable antique.

The creature was smashed to the floor, its head at a twisted angle, but it was far from giving up the fight. Scrabbling backwards, it shot up the wall toward the ceiling, trying to straighten its head with a series of dry cracks. As it did, I took the opportunity to exit my bed in a tangled vault, taking half the bedding with me.

The monstrosity launched itself at Sheila, who fended it off with a series blows like some sort of master staff-fighter while yelling at me over her shoulder. "The picture! Where is it! I couldn't find it!"

"The *what*?" I yelled back.

"The picture!" she repeated, ducking as her taloned doppelgänger swiped at her. The creature screeched, making it nearly impossible for me to think. *What the bloody hell was she talking about?*

Then it clicked. *The picture.*

The Dying Dream of Major Andre. And with it, an ugly implication: *did she come here just to steal it?*

"It's in my desk! There's a hidden compartment."

"You have to destroy it! Get it!" She ducked another swipe of the beast's claws and countered with a strike of my now-shattered antique lamp. "Burn it!"

"Are you *crazy*!?" I yelled back. It was a priceless piece of art, possibly worth millions. Sheila shot me a venomous look and for a moment I thought she was going to strike me next. Losing the sheets, I bolted through the bedroom door and down the short flight of stairs to the main room below.

Nacho was at the base of the stairs, fully arched in a classic 'cat-back' and hissing wildly as I shot past, making it to my broad banker's desk in bounds. The picture was in a secret flat file concealed in the molding of the desktop, and as I extracted it a noticed a lot of items on the desk had been moved around--had Sheila been going through my things? From upstairs came another ear-splitting screech and the sound of breaking furniture--which I feared might be another of my priceless lamps. Then I found myself in front of the fireplace, the Major's drawing in one trembling hand. I felt ridiculous standing there in my underwear with such a rare piece of art, as if such an act were, in itself, lewd and sacrilegious. Then I heard Sheila cry out as the creature flew from the bedroom door, hovering in the air at the top of the cathedral ceiling. The moonbeams angling in through the skylight gave it an even more spectral, horrific appearance and it howled as it spotted me, zooming down with the terrifying speed of a predator, fangs bared.

My hand hesitated as if in the grip of some unshakable force, the drawing inches from the glowing embers banked in the fireplace grate. My teeth were locked in grimace.

God forgive me, was all I could think.

I closed my eyes and pulled my hand *back.*

The next thing I was aware of were the icy claws gripping my neck and yanking me around like a rag doll, flinging me towards the stairs. Fortunately, my restored 1940s leather love seat stood between me and the stairs, and it toppled over as I hit it, whacking my head good on the floor as I fell for good measure. Only the padded runner saved me from a more serious injury, though I still hit hard enough to see stars.

The drawing went flying.

What followed was an odd moment, as if time slowed into a surreal crawl.

By the fireplace, I saw the creature rise up in all its majestic horror, now completely transformed into a hideous banshee. Strangely, though its eyes were but greenish orbs, I swear I was actually able to track them following the now airborne sketch by Major André as it described a fluttering see-saw arc overhead.

Down and down it went in that erratic way only a single piece of a paper can...

...and onto the head of my still arched and hissing cat, Nacho.

The reaction was instantaneous.

Even as I scrambled and leapt to save the drawing, the cat was set off as if with a cattle prod, the poor thing already a bundle of sizzling nerves. On a few occasions in the past, I'd seen what Nacho could do to a roll of toilet paper if left to his own devices . . . generally amounting to a wholesale butchery completely at odds with his usual, lazy demeanor. The dark side of Nacho, as it were.

But I'd never actually *seen* him at work until now.

Nacho flipped--quite literally--and in contrast to an entire roll of toilet paper, the obliteration of Major André's delicate drawing lasted a mere matter of seconds, in what I could only describe as an 'orgy of violence.' Shreds of paper flew every which way. Behind me, the creature shot forward as one of my hands tried instinctively to snatch at a large scrap that fluttered above the hissing/clawing/biting ball of cat and artwork.

My eardrums nearly burst from the ensuing scream, and even as the clawed hand struck at my neck, I sensed it dissolve into vaporous, icy tendrils. The echo of its last cry hovered in the room a moment longer.

Then it was over.

As if equally shocked at his own unbridled display of violence, Nacho recovered himself enough to take off in a streak of fur toward the kitchen.

The drawing was in tatters.

I blinked to see Sheila stagger out onto the landing, her hair a wild mess, the remains of the floor lamp clutched in one trembling hand.

"My lamp!" I cried.

Sheila shrugged and dropped it with a clang. "Sorry. It was either you or the Tiffany."

"I don't even know what it was . . ." I said a short while later, knees still shaking. I stood wrapped in a blanket by the fireplace (which was burning fiercely now that I'd added a few fresh logs) with a refilled snifter of Louis Royer cognac in one hand, having bolted the first one down in one gulp. Sheila stood in front of me, still in my bathrobe, hair still looking like it had been caught in a tornado, an identical snifter in her own hand. Before anything else, she'd insisted on gathering up the scraps of the drawing and putting them in the flames, even as I carried on a bit and protested.

It was beyond repair of course, but it was almost physically painful for me to see such a priceless--even if cursed--piece of artwork meet such a debasing and violent end.

"Ohhh, it was definitely some sort of Night Hag," Sheila was saying, "It was linked through the picture somehow, drawn into this existence by the Major's despair. I was told burning it was the best method to banish it, but apparently an upset housecat works just as effectively."

I was still rattled, but at least Nacho had returned and settled down again as if nothing untoward had occurred. He contemplated us from the landing with his front paws tucked in like some sort of meditating monk. I couldn't help but think he had a self-satisfied look about him, as if to say; *"Yes it was a nasty bit of business, but someone had to do it."* Still, I had to envy his way of resuming life in the moment.

On the other hand I was going to be in a whopping shit-storm when it came to explaining to the Williams family what had happened to the drawing. *Sorry folks, yes it was priceless, but then again it was possessed, and things . . . well things got a little complicated see; first the cat shredded it, then this woman I'd just picked up at a party torched what was left. So . . . any other interesting heirlooms you'd like me to look at?*

Even as I thought of it, however, a plan was taking shape. I had scanned the drawing earlier and I knew a certain 'reformed' art forger down in the city who could expertly duplicate any period style using authentic inks and papers. It would cost me, but then I could genuinely declare the drawing was in fact a cleverly done hoax . . .

That would all have to wait until later.

As Sheila pointed out, the most important thing was that I--*we*--were alive, and that trumped any dead man's artwork. She was surprisingly blunt and pragmatic about it as we straightened up the room again; "Art should be about the celebration of life, Tom. When it becomes an instrument of death, it simply has to be destroyed. There are plenty of those in the world already." Having seen what some valuables did to people's behavior, I grudgingly had to agree.

In the meantime a few other things were nagging at me.

"But this one . . . well it looked like *you*. And the one in the picture . . . it, well it looked remarkably similar to pictures I've seen of Peggy Shippen – Benedict Arnold's wife."

Sheila sipped her own cognac. I had to admit she looked good in my bathrobe. I wondered if there was any chance we could still...

"Were they having a thing going? Shippen and André?" she asked,

I thought it over. "Possibly. There were some claims he had been courting her in Philadelphia before Arnold swept in and married her."

"Well that's usually how these things work. The Night Hag, I mean. They often initially take the form of someone you desire. Not for very long--they burn up a lot of energy quickly. A psychic manifestation that flares up like gunpowder, feeding off your fears and desires. They wreak havoc very briefly. Then it goes dormant again until the next person touches the object or key, which in this case was that drawing.

"How did it, I mean, if it was connected to the drawing, how come David Williams didn't succumb? Wouldn't the curse have destroyed him?"

Sheila shook her head and crossed her arms. "No. It's not always like that. The recipient has to be emotionally vulnerable. Receptive. A die-hard pragmatist would just have had bad dreams for a couple days."

I drew up a little. "You mean to say I'm weak?"

"No, not at all," She replied, though the look on her face might have said otherwise. "These creatures are very dangerous, and sly. And you seem like a very *nice* guy."

I winced. "I don't understand. Wait, you've seen one of those things *before!?*"

"Um, not exact-well . . . yes. Actually I have. Once."

"What do you mean, *once*?"

"At a . . . well you see I'm a Wicca, and I belong to... well, I can't tell you all the details. I'm sorry, I really owe you an apology. I'm afraid none of this was an accident. I deliberately used you. I--*we*--knew about the drawing."

I shook my head, trying to make some sort of sense of what she was implying. I was already getting a sinking feeling.

"Why did you *really* come here tonight?" I said, unable to keep the edge out of my voice.

"We'd heard about the drawing and knew it had to be destroyed before anyone else got hurt. I volunteered to see what I could discover and got into the dinner tonight at the last moment. I was told to locate the drawing and, if possible, burn it. I doubt you would have just handed it to me if I'd told you all this earlier. I had to let you experience for yourself how dangerous that awful drawing was. Now you know."

I shuddered as I thought of that thing straddling me. I realized Sheila was looking at me carefully. "By the way, you didn't actually . . . you know . . .?" She made a suggestive gesture with her finger.

"Good God, no!" I stammered, "Nothing like that."

"Good," she replied. "Because that would be a little weird. And very bad. Very, *very* bad."

"Oh." I touched her shoulder, aware again how desirable she looked. "Well, that was all very exciting. Er, do you have to go just yet?"

The familiar, charming, 'realtor's' smile that appeared on her face killed any further thoughts in that direction. What she whispered next in my ear sealed it. "Thanks for the offer. But I'm afraid that, well let's just say since the divorce . . . I don't play for *your team* anymore. I should get dressed and go."

At the front door I stopped her again. "But . . . how did you . . . you looked like you'd handled that sort of thing before."

"I thought I told you I have a daughter."

Dear God I thought . . . *just what kind of kid does she have?* "Yes, a daughter. But that creature . . . ?"

Sheila smiled and moved in closer. "A Night Hag? Hell, Casey's thirteen. Going through puberty. Believe me, that was nothing."

As she stepped out into the wan light of dawn she glanced back over her shoulder almost playfully, "Good night, Tom. Be well," she said with a sparkle that matched the snow beyond her. As she found her footing on the ice, she exited with a quick swing of her hips.

I gave her a short wave, and wondered what had really transpired in my bed. It occurred to me I hadn't been altogether sure what had happened with the creature *before* I'd woken up.

However, I was certain I hadn't been physically intimate with the Night Hag.

Fairly certain, anyway.

WITHIN REACH

By David Neilsen

Albert Rosenbaum was too old for Trick-or-Treating.

His parents had been quite clear on this fact, with his mother going so far as to gently suggest that Albert didn't really need a large bag of candy and that maybe he ought to consider curbing the amount of sugar he already consumed. His father wasn't so subtle.

"Christ, lose some weight, already!"

So as Halloween approached, Albert did not spend weeks putting together a killer costume as he had in past years; he did not take an unofficial survey to determine what types of candy different houses in Philipsburg Manor would be giving away Halloween night as he had in past years; and he was not planning the most efficient route through the grid-like neighborhood to enable him to hit the maximum number of houses as he had in past years--though he still had last year's route memorized should the need arise.

Instead he sulked and nibbled on a Three Musketeers bar he had stashed under his bed. When his Mom barged into his private domain without knocking, caught him sneaking chocolate brown-handed, and cleaned out his Under-the-Bed stash he sulked even more. And dipped into his Hidden-Behind-the-Air-Vent stash.

As each day in October passed, he became more and more agitated. How in the world did they expect him to get through a Halloween without Trick-or-Treating? Sure, he was sixteen, but lots of sixteen year-olds Trick-or-Treated, didn't they? I mean what else were you supposed to do Halloween night? Stay home?

"When I was your age, we went to parties," said his Dad. "But to do that you'd need friends, so I guess you'll lock yourself in your room and play video games."

"Harold!" reprimanded Albert's Mom.

Albert kicked his Dad in the shin on his way up to his room. Once he'd calmed down with a Hershey's Special Dark, however, his mind started to go over what his Dad had said and the kernel of an idea began to form. A couple of Milky Ways later the form had evolved into a plan. A brilliant, genius, totally smart plan. A plan that just might work.

He'd lie.

"Be back by ten o'clock, honey," said Mom as Albert prepared to head out on Halloween night.

"Christ, June, it's his first real party!" barked his Dad. "Let the kid have some fun!"

Mom frowned at the rebuke, then acquiesced. "Well, maybe eleven," she relented.

"Don't come home before midnight, Al!" cheered Dad. Mom closed her eyes and gave a slight shiver, but didn't say anything.

Albert promised to be home at a reasonable--yet not too reasonable--hour and closed the door behind him, though not before longingly eyeing the family's bowl of Kit Kats and Almond Joys sitting by the door in preparation for the lucky squints due to come knocking any moment. He managed to pass by without reaching in with his sticky fingers because a) Mom and Dad were watching and b) if his plan worked he'd soon have plenty of serious candy of his own to satiate his base desires.

Stepping down the path onto Hunter Avenue, he quickly made his way to Monroe, the heart of Philipsburg Manor. He'd told his folks that his 'friend' who had invited him to this 'party' lived all the way on Merlin on the other side of the Manor, so he needed to put up a good show of jogging (well, walking a little faster than normal, anyway) down Monroe in case they were watching him through the front window. Which he knew they were. Two blocks later he crossed Harwood and knew they could no longer see him, but he kept going another block to Kelbourne because he knew a couple of the families who lived on Harwood and his plan relied on not being recognized.

Plus, Kelbourne was always a zoo. His plan would work well in a zoo.

He turned east upon hitting Kelbourne just as the first street lights flickered on in the approaching darkness and let a sloppy grin spread across his face when he saw all the various pint-sized ghosts, witches, and members of boy bands roaming from house to house filling their plastic pumpkins or pillow cases with good, honest, candy. This was going to work. He was *so* going to score.

He whipped out his official Spider Man pillow case (the Tobey Maguire version, not the stupid Andrew Garfield one) and scanned the street for his first target. This was the tricky part. It had to be believable, yet unobtrusive. He knew full well the thin line between harmless teenager and creepy stalker guy. If he didn't keep his eagerness in check, the plan would go bust in a hurry.

After considering then dismissing a few possibilities, he spotted the perfect target: three young boys, maybe ten or eleven. Old enough to be running around the Manor without a chaperone, but young enough to be totally oblivious. One kid made a pretty decent Iron Man, another a pretty lame but certainly identifiable Batman, and the third… Christ, Albert had no idea what the third kid was supposed to be. An epic fail, that's what he was.

The portly sixteen year-old strolled across the street as casually as he could until he was in position a few feet behind the three would-be superheroes. Far too involved in their candy, their costumes, and just being out alone at night, the kids ignored him and marched up the driveway to the next house. Albert followed. Waiting… waiting…

"Trick or Treat!" hollered the three pre-pubescent boys when an old woman (like his Mom's age or thereabouts) answered their pestering knock. From his spot a few feet behind the kids, watched the woman drop a handful of candy into their bags. He tensed up, knowing he'd have to time this just right, then stepped forward just as the younger boys turned around.

"You guys didn't get anything for little Jack, did you?" he asked them in a voice loud enough to be heard by the old woman at the door. As they stared at him, confused, he walked up to the door and held out his Spiderman pillow case. The candy pusher in the doorway hesitated a moment, and Albert shrugged. "Our little brother's got the flu and Mom told me to make sure they brought some candy home for him. Would you mind?"

The woman relaxed, smiled, and dropped a double handful of prime sweets into Albert's bag.

"Much obliged," he said as she closed the door in preparation for the next batch of Trick-or-Treaters to come a-pounding.

"Who's Jack?" asked Iron Man as Albert walked back through the still-confused trio. Albert just patted him on the head and kept walking.

Success! And a double-helping no less! Albert took a moment to congratulate himself on being a genius, then continued walking down the street until he hit Bellwood, already hunting for his next target. They needed to be young, but not too young. A group, but not too large a group. Someone who looked enough like him to sell the con.

And he saw them. Four little girls, a bit younger than the boys, maybe eight. Too young to be out on their own, but there were four of them and there were plenty of adults lurking about the Manor tonight, so it wasn't as if anything could happen. Albert got into position, followed unobtrusively behind them as they skipped up a walkway to the door. Waited for the schmuck at the door to hand out candy, then moved in for the kill.

Again, the girls just stared at him. Again he brazenly shoved his pillowcase at the human candy dispenser. Again he lamented about his poor, sick little brother. And again he was rewarded with a serious fistful of candy. This time the girls backed away from him as he headed back out to the street, wary and suspicious, but Albert didn't care. This evening was going better than he could have dreamed.

Albert repeated his ingenious con four more times before he started noticing some stares from folks as he passed. It seemed word of his scheme was finally spreading. Stares turned into glares and pointing as parents shunted their children away from the creepy teenager roaming the streets of Philipsburg Manor stalking little children. Albert didn't care. He had plenty of candy.

It was time to enjoy his bounty.

But he needed someplace out of the way. Someplace private. He needed to leave the Manor. Having worked his way south to Merlin during his prowl, Albert backtracked a block to Palmer and turned toward the river. When Palmer ended in a T, he then turned south into Kingsland Point Park.

Though officially closed after dark, various flickers of flashlights and a couple of tiki torches announced that tonight the park was playing host to plenty of kids of all ages. They were clumped together in tight little groups enjoying the Halloween night, both innocently and--in some cases--not so innocently. Albert kept his head down, clutched his Spider Man pillow case of candy good and tight, and speed-walked through the parking lot. The crowd thinned once he passed the small playground with its massive, demented teeth-shaped edifices jutting from the ground and vanished altogether when reached the cordoned-off path leading along the shore to the lighthouse.

Albert took a quick look around, making sure he was away from any prying eyes, then quickly ducked past the never-locked chain-link gate and onto the old GM property. The massive automotive factory had been the lifeblood of the village of Sleepy Hollow for generations, but after closing in the early 90's, the buildings had all been torn down leaving an empty, weed-choked, post-industrial wasteland right on the river. A deal to turn the property into a thriving residential and commercial development called Lighthouse Landing had recently been announced, but that was still a decade away.

The debris and detritus of twenty years provided Albert with adequate shelter, and he soon found himself a good, out-of-the-way spot to settle down and gorge on his haul. Twin mountain ranges of dirt had created a small, hidden valley surrounding a round drainage grate in the endless plains of concrete. Albert plopped down beside the grate (which promised to be a perfect place to toss away the evidence of his crimes) and went to work. He dumped his massive hoard on the ground and by the light of the moon picked out all the lame candy--gum, brandless hard candy, and a couple of candy canes obviously left over from last Christmas. These quickly found their way into the oblivion beneath the grate. Next, he dug into the appetizers: 'fun-sized' Snickers, Twix bars, and Kit Kats. M&Ms. Whoppers. Barely worth the time it took to unwrap, Albert popped down his throat with a satisfied gasp, like a parched man in the desert taking that first sip of lukewarm water.

The wrappers from these dainty morsels followed the banished candy into the dark, bottomless void under the metal grate as the mother of all Sugar Buzzes slowly formed within Albert's overweight frame. Nerve endings tingled, eyes twitched, heart raced. Still he ate. Now he was pulling out the big guns. Full-sized chocolate bars. An Almond Joy. A Baby Ruth. A Hershey's Cookies 'n' Cream. By now, his fingers and toes could simply not stay still. Freeing the glorious chocolate bars from their wrappers became harder and harder. Still, he would not stop. Not until every last prize had been consumed.

The gastrointestinal carnage lasted a relatively brief amount of time, all things considered. In less than ten minutes, all that remained to be consumed was the purest of the pure: a king-sized Hershey's Milk Chocolate bar. Albert's meaty fingers grasped for the small slice of chocolate gold, twitching and shaking from the mad rush of sugar coursing through his veins. It took Albert three tries to successfully pick it up, so frazzled and frenetic were his limbs and appendages. But he was nothing if not determined to devour this final, magnificent, bar as if it were manna from Heaven.

And then he dropped it.

Albert's eyes bugged out and his unnaturally-vibrating heart skipped a beat as he watched his treasure slip from his grasp and dive down through the bars of the metal grate into the inky blackness beyond.

"No!!!!!"

Ignoring his shivers, he rolled onto his knees and dug his fat fingers between the bars in a futile effort to retrieve the prize he had lost. Unfortunately, they simply did not fit into the tight space between the bars of the grate.

"No! No, no, no! Come back!"

He punched the grate again and again in frustration, his sugar buzz preventing his knuckles from feeling pain as they rapped repeatedly on the solid steel bars. He felt imprisoned, the cold, metal bars cutting him off from the freedom of his well-earned chocolate. Sealing his doom. It wasn't fair. He had done it! He had tricked homeowners and treated himself to a lavish supply of candy. He'd earned that candy bar fair and square!

Then he had to go and fumble the damn thing.

He gave the grate another try, hoping to squeeze his puffy wrists through the bars. No dice. Next, he tried to pry the damn thing up. There was movement, but he couldn't get a firm grip on the bars.

What he needed was something he could jam in there to give himself some leverage. A crow bar or a big screwdriver. He looked around his little valley in the faint, ghoulish moonlight and his eyes rested on a long, metal pipe. It would be awkward and clumsy, but it was better than nothing.

Jamming the pipe between the bars, he pulled back and was rewarded by a groan of metal as the grate slowly rose. Then the tip of the pipe slipped and the grate slammed back into place.

"God... stupid.... ghaaa!"

Far below, something stirred.

Determined, Albert rammed the pipe in deeper and eventually, with much grunting and groaning, pried the grate up and out. It clanged to the side and out of the way, revealing a dark, black aperture maybe a foot in diameter.

He quickly got down on his stomach and rammed his arm into the void, disturbing a decade's worth of dust.

Something felt the first stirrings of a breeze in its limited existence.

Albert's fingers explored the dark abyss but failed to find his prize. He shifted his weight and lunged deeper into the beckoning darkness, shoving his head inside until only the flabby width of his shoulders kept him from being sucked down into the blackness. The subterranean heat brought beads of sweat to his face. He shook them off while extending his arm down into the stygian depths, causing them to plop down into the fetid deep one by one.

Something greedily sucked in the warm moisture raining down from above.

With his body cutting off what little light there was, Albert closed his useless eyes and concentrated on his sense of touch. He reached an instant of manic jubilation as his fingers scraped against a ledge, then fell into an equally manic despair as he found no trace of his precious confection.

Frustrated, he slammed his hand against one of the many pipes with an audible clang.

Something heard the clang and throbbed its way towards the sound.

Albert's breath now came in fits and starts, and he fought back a rising panic of suffocation. He twisted and contorted his shoulders, scraping them raw against the sides of the opening to gain just one more inch of reach.

Something felt Albert's fingertips flit across its surface.

Albert jerked his hand away. It had felt stringy and veiny and slightly furry and utterly disgusting. Hesitating but a moment, he shook his head clear and reached out in the opposite direction.

His fingers brushed against the stringy, veiny, slightly furry something again and he spasmed away in revulsion.

Fear building to a climax, Albert was paralyzed a moment between the need to get his chocolate and the need to get away from whatever was down there.

A moment was all it took.

Suddenly, a nasty, slimy, fuzzy *something* wrapped itself around his fingers.

"Christ!" screamed Albert, his voice echoing into the depths of the void below. He instinctively pulled away, but his shoulder was so well jammed into the hole that he was unable to escape. As the tendrils of the something climbed up his elbow and forearm, the poor boy's mind snapped in terror and he opened his mouth to scream.

And something gleefully plunged into the warm, moist cavern, which had suddenly appeared.

Albert's body bucked and bolted as the something forced its way down his throat. His systems shut down one by one in response to the foreign invader, and repeated convulsions thrashed him about mindlessly. The something held fast to his arm as it spread inside its newfound womb of flesh, poking holes in the flimsy walls between internal organs.

One final, extremely violent fit yanked Albert's shoulder out of the hole and he fell up and back, bringing his body once again into the light. For an instant, a thin, green vine could be seen stretching from Albert's mouth down into the darkness. Then a massive coughing spasm ejected the tendril from his body and back down into the waiting abyss.

Albert immediately rolled onto trembling hands and knees as his guts poured out of his mouth, fragments of internal organs mixing with a mass of deep red blood on the cement.

Albert Rosenbaum would be dead within ten minutes.

The seed pods planted within him would survive on his bloated corpse until strong enough to hatch from his flesh and survive on their own, albeit in their dormant larval stage.

Then they would wait.

In a few years, the first of many fertile fields of flesh would move into the new luxury apartments making up the planned community of Lighthouse Landing.

And the waiting would be over.

THOSE RESPONSIBLE

Washington Irving was born in 1783 and died in 1859. Between those years he accomplished more than you ever will, and he feels quite pleased about that. Considered by many as the first great American author, he is perhaps most famous for his short stories "The Legend of Sleepy Hollow" and "Rip Van Winkle." Though it comes as a shock to many to discover, the truth is he actually wrote quite a number of other things, such as historical works on the lives of George Washington, Oliver Goldsmith, and Muhammad, but nobody really cares much about those anymore. He was first published in 1802 and continued to successfully write and publish up to his death 57 years later in Tarrytown. He was also the U.S. ambassador to Spain from 1842 to 1846, but then who wasn't? Right?

He continued to write after his death, and his posthumous work in what critics have labeled "Erotica of Manners" proved wildly successful. His foray into film has not been as successful as his literary works, the highlight being his co-writing credit on 1991's 'Teenage Mutant Ninja Turtles II: The Secret of the Ooze.'

Born an army brat in El Paso, Texas and raised in Westchester County, New York, ***Jonathan Kruk*** grew up on tall tales and daydreams. Telling tales to his kid brother led to a career as a full time storyteller. He performed Ritual Urban Theater with Gabrielle

Roth, and entertained at more than 1,000 children's birthday parties. Freeport Schools, on Long Island made him storyteller-in-residence, after which he began to perform full-time.

Now he enchants children every year at hundreds of schools, libraries, historic sites and festivals performing finger fables, story theater and New York lore. Jonathan is best known for one man performances of "The Legend of Sleepy Hollow" and "A Christmas Carol" for Historic Hudson Valley. Parents Choice and the National Association of Parenting Publications gave Jonathan's CD of the headless horseman their Silver Medal and Honors awards, and Hudson Valley Magazine selected Jonathan as "Best Storyteller in the Hudson Valley." His book "Legends and Lore of Sleepy Hollow and the Hudson Valley" was published in 2011 by The History Press.

Christine Morgan works the overnight shift in a psychiatric facility, which plays havoc with her sleep schedule but allows her a lot of writing time. A lifelong reader, she also reviews, beta-reads, occasionally edits, and dabbles in self-publishing. Her other interests include gaming, history, superheroes, crafts, cheesy disaster movies and training to be a crazy cat lady. She can be found online at https://www.facebook.com/christinemorganauthor and https://christinemariemorgan.wordpress.com/

Having been born and raised in Kinderhook, NY, the town where Washington Irving penned portions of 'The Legend of Sleepy Hollow,' it is perhaps no surprise that *Scott J Laurange* found himself from an early age drawn to the supernatural and the macabre. Thus steeped in the history of American gothic literature, it was inevitable that he would add his humble voice to that mighty chorus that resounds through the ages. His unhealthy love of disco, his wacky sensibility, and his incorrigible pomposity permeate his unusual take on the genre. He currently resides in Texas with his wife, son, and four cats. He can be found online at https://scottjlaurange.wordpress.com/.

James C. Simpson is a mysterious recluse from the wild mountains of Pennsylvania. He has had a lifelong fascination with the macabre, being particularly keen to the Gothic masters. When he is not writing a new tale of terror, he often finds himself enjoying the solitude of nature or the darkened realm of the cinema. He has been published multiple times, both in print and digitally.

Born in Roanoke, Virginia, in the bicentennial year, **Ezra Heilman** is a writer and educator. He holds degrees in music and linguistics from Jacksonville University and Cal State Fullerton, respectively. When he's not reading, writing, or correcting student essays, he plays classical flute and tweets. He currently resides with his wife in Pasadena, California. He owns no cats, but he promises he likes them. You can follow Ezra on Twitter at @EzraHeilman or on his blog at autumnalscribe.blogspot.com.

B.B. Stucco lives a miserly existence hidden away in the jungles of deepest Sleepy Hollow. In addition to shamelessly adapting pre-existing folk tales into startling tales of impropriety, he works as both a paragon of virtue and as an example of uncommon manliness Born independently wealthy, thanks to his family's dominance in the inflatable dalmatian industry, his lifelong ambition has long been to have a short story published in an anthology dedicated to the mysterious land he loves.

Now that this has been accomplished, he knows not what adventure he shall embark upon next nor where the winds of fate shall blow him. Perhaps he shall watch some television. Perhaps not.

A native of England, ***Andrew M. Seddon*** spent a number of his formative years in upstate New York, which included, at some point, a visit to Sleepy Hollow. He has over one hundred fifty publication credits, and enjoys writing in the genres of science fiction, historical fiction (particularly the Roman era), and ghost and horror stories. The author of six books, his most recent is "Ring of Time" (Splashdown Books 2014). His next science fiction novel, "The DeathCats of Asa'ican and Other Tales of A Space Vet," is due from Splashdown Books in 2015.

He is an active member of Science Fiction and Fantasy Writers of America and the Authors' Guild, and when not writing he can be found hiking, enjoying classical music, and running marathons. He lives in Montana and Florida with his wife Olivia and German Shepherd, Rex.

In his professional life, ***Michael Nayak*** is a rocket scientist who has worked on the Space Shuttle and two-probe NASA missions to the moon, and as Flight Director for multiple experimental satellites. Outside work, he instructs skydiving, high performance parachuting, and vertical wind tunnel flying, and he owns a small aerospace consulting firm. When he's not writing, Michael is an avid motorcycle rider, skier, scuba diver and pilot. Originally from Los Angeles, he now lives in the San Francisco Bay area, where he is working on his first novel and a PhD in Planetary Science.

His fiction has appeared in several anthologies that include "Girl at the End of the World" (Fox Books) and "Triangulation: Lost Voices" (Parsec Ink). Visit his Amazon Author page at www.amazon.com/author/nayak.

Amy Braun is a Canadian urban fantasy and horror author. Her work revolves around monsters, magic, mythology, and mayhem. She has been featured on various author blogs and publishing websites, is an active member of the Writing GIAM community, participates in NaNoWriMo, and is the recipient of April Moon Books Editor Award for "author voice, world-building and general bad-assery."

When she isn't writing, she's reading, watching movies, taking photos, gaming, and struggling with chocoholism and ice cream addiction. Amy's current work includes various short stories such as "Hotel Hell" and "Call From The Grave," the full length novels "Cursed: Demon's Daughter" and "Path of the Horseman," and the novella "Needfire." Amy can be found online through her frequently updated blog, Literary Braun (literarybraun.blogspot.ca), as well as on Twitter (@amybraunauthor) and Facebook (facebook.com/amybraunauthor).

Robert Stava is a writer who now lives in the lower Hudson Valley just north of NYC, apparently not far from that half-imaginary village he sets so many of his stories in: Wyvern Falls. Originally from Cleveland, Ohio, he grew up in the Finger Lakes region of New York State, and after pursuing a degree in Fine Arts wound up making his career as a 'Mad Man' in advertising at Y&R and J. Walter Thompson in NYC. He went on to become a multimedia Art Director, and later as Creative Director ran the 3d Media Group at Arup--an international U.K-based design and engineering company--before catapulting into the wild world of writing horror fiction.

Author of the novels "At Van Eyckmann's Request" and "The Feast of Saint Anne," his first published short story "Municipal Lot #9" appeared in issue 017 of Sanitarium Magazine. His novella "The Devil's Engine" will be released from Muzzleland Press in August, 2015. The third novel in his "Hudson Horror" novels, "By Summer's Last Twilight," is due out in autumn of 2015. He is also author and designer of "Combat Recon: 5th Air Force Images from the SW Pacific 1943-45" (Schiffer Publishing, 2007), a historical account based around his great uncle's service as a combat photographer during WWII.

David Neilsen is the author of a number of slightly disturbing short stories that have been published in various anthologies as well as online. His debut novel, the middle grade horror story "Doctor Fell and the Playground of Doom," will be published by Crown Books for Young Readers in August 2016. He spent a dozen years working in Hollywood, culminating in optioning a pilot to 20th Century Fox (that went nowhere), and penning the screenplay for the Straight-to-DVD film "The Eliminator" (rent it, he dares you).

David is also a professional storyteller based in Sleepy Hollow who has inadvertently given children nightmares at such locations a Sleepy Hollow Cemetery, Washington Irving's Sunnyside, and The New York Botanical Gardens. His one-man performances based on the work of H.P. Lovecraft have spread joy and madness throughou the northeast. For more information on David's work, visit him online at http://neilsenparty.wordpress.com.

ACKNOWLEDGMENTS

First, I must thank the incomparable Jerry Carrino for taking the time to read and edit the words within out of the goodness of his own heart and a penchant for self-punishment. Also, a huge thank you goes to the amazingly-talented Luke Spooner for his wonderful cover art, which perfectly encapsulates the emotion and atmosphere of this collection.

Thank you, also, to all of my models who had literally no idea what was going on when I swooped in and took a picture. Max, Rachel, Peter, Mom, Nick, you were all fantastic.

I also need to thank Jessica Burke and Anthony Burdge of Myth Ink Books for their help and guidance in the early phases of this project.

Finally, I'd like to thank all of the wonderful writers who submitted stories to this anthology. It was a joy to read so many different tales of the region, and you made the selection process incredibly difficult.

Made in the USA
Middletown, DE
14 October 2015